'No,' Mike ground out as he carried her from the kitchen in the direction of the bedroom. 'That is *not* what I want. I just want *you*, Natalie.'

Natalie didn't say a word as he swept her into the bedroom. She was too busy fighting with the futile hopes that his passionate words evoked in her.

Because he didn't *really* want her, did he? Not for for ever. Just for the time being.

But the time being *was* exciting, she told herself as he lowered her to the bed.

*Enjoy it, Natalie.*

And who knew what might happen in the future?

# WIVES WANTED

**When a wealthy man wants a wife,
he doesn't always follow the rules!**

Welcome to Miranda Lee's stunning, sexy new trilogy

Meet Richard, Reece and Mike, three Sydney
millionaires with a mission—they all want to get
married…but none wants to fall in love!

## BOUGHT: ONE BRIDE

Richard's story:

**His money can buy him anything he wants…
and he wants a wife!**

July 2005

## THE TYCOON'S TROPHY WIFE

Reece's story:

**She was everything he wanted in a wife…
till he fell in love with her!**

October 2005

## A SCANDALOUS MARRIAGE

Mike's story:

**He married her for money—her beauty was a bonus!**

November 2005

# A SCANDALOUS
# MARRIAGE

BY
MIRANDA LEE

MILLS & BOON®

First published in Great Britain 2005
Harlequin Mills & Boon Limited,
Eton House, 18-24 Paradise Road, Richmond, Surrey TW9 1SR

© Miranda Lee 2005

ISBN 0 263 84192 8

Set in Times Roman 10½ on 13 pt.
01-1105-38532

Printed and bound in Spain
by Litografia Rosés, S.A., Barcelona

# CHAPTER ONE

MIKE was grimly silent during the taxi ride from Mascot to his apartment in Glebe. He wasn't at all happy with the way his business trip to the States had turned out, or the course of action he'd rather impulsively decided to take.

But it was too late to change his mind now. He was locked in.

Once home, Mike stripped off the Italian business suit that he'd bought for his meeting with Helsinger and headed for the bathroom. After a shower and shave, he pulled on blue jeans and a T-shirt, then set about cooking himself a decent breakfast. The breakfast they'd served him on the plane as they'd approached Sydney hadn't touched his sides.

Mike ate the plate of bacon and eggs out on the sun-drenched balcony, which was north-facing and had a great view of Sydney's inner harbour.

The balcony was one of the reasons Mike had bought this particular apartment. Water relaxed him, he'd discovered. He liked nothing better than to sit out here in the evening after a hard day's work on the computer, sipping a glass of whisky whilst the water distracted and calmed his mind.

Nothing, however, was going to calm his mind at this moment.

He ate quickly, his aim just to fill his stomach before driving into the city to meet with his best friend—and banker. As Mike scraped the leftovers into the garbage disposal he wondered what Richard's reaction would be.

Mike suspected he'd be supportive of his rather unconventional decision. Richard might look conservative, but underneath he was anything but. You didn't get to be CEO of an international bank before the age of forty by being meek and mild. Richard had his ruthless side, especially when it came to making money. And as crazy as Mike's scheme might sound, if it succeeded, it was going to make both of them very wealthy men.

Five minutes later, Mike slipped on his favourite black leather jacket and headed for the front door. Half an hour later, he was sitting in Richard's office.

'What do you mean you didn't see Helsinger?' Richard's tone was more confused than angry. 'I thought you'd lined that meeting up before you left Sydney.'

'Unfortunately, Chuck was called out of town the day I arrived in LA,' Mike told him. 'He left his apologies. A family emergency.'

'Hell, Mike. That was bad luck.'

'No sweat. I met with his managing director, instead. He assured me Comproware were still very interested in my new anti-virus, anti-spyware program.'

'Yes, I'm sure they are,' Richard said drily. 'It's brilliant.'

Mike wholeheartedly agreed with Richard. It *was* brilliant, especially the way it could track back to see where the virus—or the spy—came from, then deliver a counter-strike of its own. Mike had known, right from the first day he'd started work on the ground-breaking program, that his own relatively small, Australian-based software company didn't have the power to do such a product justice. He needed an international company with marketing clout to launch it, worldwide.

After doing some indepth research, he'd come up with Comproware, a relatively new American soft-ware company that had great marketing flair, and which also had a reputation for offering generous con-tracts to the creators of new programs and games, paying royalties instead of a flat sum.

After some not-so-successful negotiating via the in-ternet and the telephone, Mike had flown to Comproware's head office in America to meet the owner face to face. He'd expected to pin Helsinger down to a contract during his two-day stopover. He certainly hadn't expected what had transpired, or the path he'd now set himself upon.

'I didn't get a contract,' he admitted. 'What I did get, however, was the offer of a possible partnership.'

'A partnership!' Richard exclaimed excitedly. 'With Chuck Helsinger? You've got to be kidding. That man's a retail legend. Everything he touches turns to gold. A partnership with him has to be worth millions.'

'Actually, Rich, more like billions. If I can close

this deal, your fifteen per cent of my little company is going to make you an even richer man than you already are. Reece is going to be pretty pleased with his fifteen per cent, too.'

And *my* seventy per cent share means I'm going to be able to do all those things I've always wanted to do, Mike thought, not for the first time. A boys' club in every city and big town in Australia. Lots more summer camps. And scholarships.

The possibilities were limitless!

*If* he got the partnership.

Richard shook his head in amazement. 'I can't believe it. This is incredible.'

'There was one small catch. But I can fix that.'

Richard immediately looked wary. 'What catch?'

'Chuck Helsinger has a hard-and-fast rule about the men he goes into partnership with.'

'What rule is that?'

'They have to be married. Settled men with solid family values.'

'You're joking.'

'Nope.'

Richard groaned, then leant back in his leather office chair, his elbows on the padded arm-rests, his hands steepled together in front, his dark brows drawing together. 'And how, pray tell, are you going to fix that?'

'I've already started. I immediately emailed Chuck that I'd recently become engaged to a wonderful girl and that we were getting married before Christmas.'

Richard's eyebrows formed a sardonic arch. 'That

was very inventive of you, Mike, but I don't think that's going to cut it. A man like Chuck Helsinger is sure to have any prospective business partner of his thoroughly investigated. He'll soon find out that you lied to him.'

'I did think of that. But it's not going to be a lie for long.'

Richard shot forward on his chair. 'You mean you'd actually get married!'

Mike could understand his friend's shock. Mike was, after all, a confirmed bachelor. He'd told Richard many times that marriage would never be on his agenda.

Still, he'd never anticipated a deal such as this coming his way. Sometimes, a man had to do what a man had to do.

But on his own terms, of course.

'If I want this partnership,' Mike said matter-of-factly, 'I'm going to have to. And as soon as possible. Helsinger is going to be in Sydney on the fourth of December to pick up a luxury yacht he's having built here. It's a Christmas present for his family. He and his wife want me and my new bride to join them for a couple of days for a getting-to-know-you cruise around Sydney's waterways. I presume, if I pass muster as a happily married man with solid family values, the partnership will be mine.'

'Good God!' Richard exclaimed.

'Look, I don't intend to *stay* married,' Mike informed his friend. 'It will just be a business arrangement, played out till the partnership is signed and sealed.'

'That's a bit cold-blooded, isn't it, Mike? Even for you.'

Mike shrugged. 'The end justifies the means. After all, what right does that hypocritical old buzzard have to insist on such a ridiculous requirement? Being married has nothing to do with being a good businessman. I'm proof of that.'

'Maybe, but that doesn't make him hypocritical.'

'You reckon? I did some investigating myself before I decided on Comproware, delving into its owner's professional and personal background. Did you know that Chuck's on his third wife, a woman, I might add, who's a good twenty-five years younger than his own seventy years? Okay, so they *have* been married for sixteen years and she's given him children. Two boys. But does that make him a decent man with solid family values?'

'I see what you mean,' Richard muttered.

'His wife can't be much better. Do you honestly think she married him for his charm? Hell, no. She hitched herself to a gravy train, like lots of women do with wealthy guys. You know how it is, Rich. Money is one hell of an incentive when it comes to some members of the fairer sex. Since I became a millionaire, I've never been lacking for female company. I'll have no trouble finding myself a temporary wife. I just have to wave the right amount under the right girl's mercenary little nose.'

'You sound like you have someone in mind. One

of your ex-girlfriends, I suppose. You've had enough of them.'

'Hell, no. None of those will do. The last thing I want is complications, or consequences. I need a wife who knows exactly what I require from her, right from the start. Which is absolutely nothing but appearances. This will be a marriage in name only, to be discreetly dissolved at a later date. There will be no consummation of this union. Be assured of that!' Mike finished up forcefully.

He was sick and tired of women claiming emotional involvement with him, despite his up-front warnings. They seemed to accept his 'just-company-and-sex' rule to begin with. But once he took them to bed a few times, they changed. Mike couldn't bear it when a woman started telling him she loved him. For one thing, he just didn't believe them. Women trotted out those three little words all the time to manipulate men. And to try to trap them.

Little did they know that telling Mike they loved him was the kiss of death.

That was the reason for his many exes. As soon as they began to get clingy, that was it. His latest ex had been a dedicated career girl. A lawyer, chosen because he'd thought she might be different. But no…she'd soon become just as possessive as all the others.

Mike had given up dating for a while, because he simply couldn't stand the scenes. Lately, he'd been spending his spare time with his charity work, instead. And putting in more hours at the gym.

'And where do you think you're going to find this super mercenary creature, Mike? Girls don't walk around with signs on them saying they'll marry for money.'

'What a short memory you have, Rich. I'll get her from an internet introduction agency, of course. Didn't you tell me yourself that you tried Wives Wanted before you found Holly? And didn't you confess to me over a bottle of Johnny Walker that that particular matchmaking service had loads of good-looking gold-diggers on their books?'

Richard frowned. 'You're right. I did say that. But, in hindsight, maybe I misjudged them. I was in a pretty cynical state of mind at the time I dated those women. They probably weren't as bad as all that. I mean, Reece found Alanna using that agency. No one in their right minds would call her a gold-digger.'

'There are always the exception to the rule,' Mike said, his mind momentarily going to Reece's lovely and very loving wife. 'Alanna is that exception. Wives Wanted will have what I'm looking for. What I need from you, Rich, is their contact number. Do you still have it? If you don't, I could ask Reece.'

'I have it here somewhere,' Richard admitted.

No use protesting further, he realised as he opened the top drawer in his desk and went through the pile of business cards he kept in the corner, looking for the one from Wives Wanted. Mike was clearly determined to do this. And who could blame him? A partnership with Chuck Helsinger was the chance of a lifetime.

Still…

Holly wasn't going to believe him when he told her about this tonight. Mike was the most anti-marriage guy they knew. Anti-marriage. Anti-love. And anti-women.

No, that was going too far. He wasn't anti-women. There was always some beautiful dolly-bird on his arm. Women buzzed around Mike like bees to the honeypot. Richard wasn't too sure why, since Mike wasn't conventionally handsome. Holly said it was because he was tall, dark and dangerous-looking.

Richard conceded that Mike's macho appearance might be the main contributing factor to his attractiveness. He had wall-to-wall muscles. And then some.

He also rarely dressed in suits, favouring jeans and leather jackets. Black, like the one he had on today.

Whatever it was, Mike was never lacking in female company. Fortunately, Holly didn't go for that type. She preferred his own more conservative, well-groomed style. Thank God.

'Here it is,' he said as he picked up the card and handed it across to Mike. 'The woman who runs the place is called Natalie Fairlane. Her name and number are on the back. She'll want you to come in for an interview before she matches you up with anyone. She never takes on a client over the internet. I suggest you don't tell her up front what your agenda is. Ms Fairlane takes her matchmaking services very seriously. One other little word of warning, too. The women on the Wives Wanted database whom I dated were all drop dead gorgeous. It might be wise if you didn't pick one who's too beautiful. Otherwise, it could be hard for a man like you to keep your hands off.'

Mike bristled. 'What do you mean, a man like me?'

'You like your sex, Mike. Don't pretend you don't. You've had more girlfriends in the few years I've known you than the stock market has ups and down. I think you're very wise not consummating this marriage. But will you be able to resist temptation? The reality is that during the time that you're going to be…"married"—' Richard made quotation-like signs with his fingers '—you and your new bride will be together quite a bit. You'll have to share a cabin on Helsinger's yacht, for starters. If she's too pretty, you might find it hard to keep your hands off the merchandise.'

'You underestimate me, Rich. I can do celibate. No problem.' He'd been doing it for a few weeks now. 'For the amount of money at stake here, I'd become a monk for life.'

Richard didn't look too convinced. 'If you say so. Now don't forget what I said about Natalie Fairlane,' he added when Mike stood up. 'Watch what you say to her.'

'I think you're being a bit naïve about the owner of Wives Wanted,' Mike replied. 'Ms Fairlane is in the marriage business strictly for the money, just like ninety-nine per cent of her female clients. Wave the right amount under *her* nose and the old bag'll find me the right girl before you can say Jack Robinson.'

A wry smile pulled at Richard's mouth as he watched Mike leave. He'd love to be a fly on the wall when his friend met the formidable Ms Fairlane.

Mike might be right about her being as mercenary as some of the women on the Wives Wanted database. He didn't know her well enough to judge. But an old bag, she was not.

# CHAPTER TWO

'MUM, this is terrible,' Natalie said. 'How on earth did you and Dad let your finances get into such a mess?'

Even as she asked the question Natalie already knew the answer. Her father had always been attracted to get-rich-quick schemes. He wasn't a gambler in the ordinary sense of the word. He didn't waste money at casinos or on the racetrack, but he was a sucker for the kind of investment or business idea that sounded too good to be true, and usually was.

Natalie hadn't realised what a poor businessman he'd been when she'd been growing up. She'd never lacked for anything. As an only child, she'd actually been rather spoilt.

It wasn't till Natalie had grown up that she'd realised her parents lived mainly on credit.

She'd been helping her mother out with her housekeeping budget for quite some time—slipping her a hundred dollars or so every time they saw each other. But now, it seemed that things had really hit rock-bottom. Her father could no longer continue with his latest venture—a lawn-mowing franchise he'd foolishly borrowed money on top of his already hefty mortgage to buy, and which required a fit young man to run.

Natalie's dad was reasonably fit. But he was fifty-seven.

Last month, he'd fallen and broken his ankle. Naturally, he hadn't taken out any income-protection insurance. What sane insurance company would have given it to him, anyway?

The bank was threatening to repossess their house if they didn't meet their mortgage, which was already running months in arrears. Natalie could cover a couple of months' payments, but not the many thousands of dollars they were behind.

Which meant her parents would shortly have no money and no place to live.

Natalie shuddered at the thought of having them live with her. She was thirty-four years of age, long past the time when you enjoyed living with your parents.

On top of that, she ran her business from home, using one of the two bedrooms in her terraced house as an office-cum-computer room, and her downstairs living room as her reception and interviewing area. Things would get very difficult with two more adults in the place. Especially two miserable ones.

'Don't you worry, dear,' her mother said. 'I'm going to get a job.'

Natalie rolled her eyes. Her mother was as big a dreamer as her father. She hadn't been properly employed for over twenty years. She'd been busy helping her silly husband with all his crazy schemes. On top of that, she was even older than Natalie's dad.

No one was going to employ a fifty-nine-year-old woman with no certifiable qualifications.

'Don't be ridiculous, Mum,' Natalie said more sharply than she intended. 'It's not that easy to get a job at your age.'

'I'm going to do cleaning. Your father ran off some fliers on that old computer and printer you gave him and I put them in every postbox in the neighbourhood.'

Natalie wanted to cry. It wasn't right that her mother had to become a cleaner at her age.

'Mum, I could get a second mortgage on this place,' Natalie offered. 'It's gone up quite a bit in value since I bought it.'

'You'll do no such thing,' her mother said firmly. 'We'll be fine. I don't want you to worry.'

Then why did you tell me? Natalie groaned silently.

The sound of her doorbell ringing brought Natalie back to her own life. 'Mum, can I ring you back later? I have a client at the door.' Her first in a fortnight. Business at Wives Wanted had dropped off a bit this past month. She hadn't had any new female clients, either. Maybe it was time for another series of magazine ads. It was a rare business that could survive on word of mouth alone.

'You go, dear. But do ring me back later.'

'I will. I promise.'

Natalie hung up quickly, buttoning up her suit jacket as she rose and headed for the front door.

A quick glance in the hallway mirror as she passed

by assured her she looked every inch the professional businesswoman. Her thick auburn hair was pulled back tightly into a French pleat. Her make-up was minimal and her jewellery discreet. Just a slimline gold wrist-watch and simple gold studs in her ears.

It wasn't till her hand reached for the knob that Natalie wondered what Mr Mike Stone looked like.

He'd been referred to her by Richard Crawford, a merchant banker who'd been a client of Wives Wanted earlier this year. Natalie suspected, however, that Mr Stone wasn't in the banking business. He hadn't sounded like executive material over the phone. He'd sounded less polished than Richard Crawford. Hopefully, that didn't mean less rich. Most of her male clients were well-off, professional men.

But beggars couldn't be choosers, especially not right now. If Mr Stone was willing to pay a few thousand for her to find him a wife, then he could be a truck driver for all she cared.

Better, however, if he were a *rich* truck driver. Most of her girls weren't in the market for working-class husbands.

Natalie turned the knob and opened the front door, her eyes widening when she saw the man standing on her doorstep.

Never, during the three years she'd been running Wives Wanted, had she had a client quite like this.

He wouldn't have looked totally out of place behind the wheel of a truck, she supposed. Not if it was an army truck and he was wearing a military uniform instead of the jeans and black leather jacket he was currently wearing.

Mike Stone was soldier material through and through.

Not an ordinary soldier, Natalie decided as her assessing gaze travelled all the way up his impressive body to his hard, dark eyes and close-cropped brown hair. A commando, one of those highly trained soldiers who went on covert missions and killed people without making a sound or turning a hair's breadth.

He wasn't classically good-looking. His features lacked symmetry. His nose had obviously been broken at one stage and his mouth was way too cruel.

But, for all that, Natalie found him extremely attractive.

Natalie smothered an inner sigh of frustration, at the same time making sure that not a single hint of interest showed on her face.

Ever since she could remember, Natalie had been attracted to men like this. Men who didn't fit the conventional mould. Men who exuded an air of danger. Men who both intrigued and aroused her.

Ten years ago, she would have gone openly gaga over this guy. Today, the inner twanging of her female antennae irritated the life out of her.

'Ms Fairlane?' he enquired, his rough, gravelly voice matching his appearance.

'Yes,' she returned, annoyed with the way her heart was racing. And with the way *he* was looking *her* up and down, his expression somewhat surprised. What on earth had Richard Crawford told him about her?

'Mike Stone,' he said at last, and held out his hand.

She hesitated before she placed her own hand in his, steeling herself not to react to his touch in any way.

But when his large male fingers closed firmly around her much smaller, softer hand, there it was. That spark. That automatic zap of sexual chemistry, running up her arm, leaving goose-bumps in the wake of its highly charged current.

Thank God her jacket had long sleeves, and that she had anticipated something like this.

'Pleased to meet you, Mr Stone,' she said, her outer coolness belying her inner heat. If she'd met Mike Stone anywhere else, she would have walked away. No, she would have *run*. But she could hardly do so at this moment. He was a potential paying client. A potential five grand in her pocket. Money she was in desperate need of today.

'Mike,' he said. 'Call me Mike.'

'Mike,' she repeated, her mouth pulling back into a plastic smile. 'Well, come on in, Mike,' she said, waving him past her into the hallway. 'The first room on the left. Go right in and find a place to sit.'

Natalie pressed herself hard against the wall as he stepped inside. No way did she want his broad-shouldered body accidentally brushing against her chest as he walked along the narrow hallway. But once he did move safely past her, she watched his back view far too avidly and for far too long before she pulled herself together and flung the front door shut, rolling her eyes at herself as she followed him into the living room.

By this time he was settling himself in the middle of her sofa, his long legs stretching out in front of him whilst he leant back and glanced around.

Natalie knew it was an oddly furnished room, filled with pieces that didn't match but that she personally liked. There were three large squashy armchairs covered in an assortment of prints, plus a seductively long brown velvet sofa, which stretched across under the front window and on which her client had just made himself very comfortable.

On the wall opposite the sofa was a state-of-the-art home theatre system, which she was still paying for. The wall to the right of her visitor had built-in floor-to-ceiling bookshelves, in front of which sat an ancient mahogany desk, with the latest laptop sitting on one end and an old-fashioned green desk lamp on the other. The floor was polished boxwood, a colourful circular rug providing warmth and a touch of the orient.

There was no coffee-table to bump into, just an assortment of side tables in all shapes and sizes on which sat ornaments and curios bought from flea markets and garage sales. Two standing lamps with gold-fringed lampshades flanked the sofa, providing subtle light at night when she was watching TV.

A friend had once commented to Natalie that the décor of her living room was very much as she was. Hard to pin down.

'You're very punctual,' she said brusquely, glancing at her watch as she headed for the upright chair behind her desk. It was right on five, the time they'd agreed upon for his interview.

'I'm always punctual when I'm not working,' he replied.

Natalie ground to an instant halt. 'I'm sorry,' she said sharply. 'But I don't take on male clients who are unemployed.'

Again, he looked her up and down, his expression this time annoyingly unreadable.

'I didn't say I was unemployed. I said I wasn't working at the moment. I am self-employed. I own a computer software company.'

Natalie could not have been more surprised. He didn't look at all like a man who spent most of his life sitting at a computer. He was far too fit-looking. Far too tanned.

As Brandon had been.

His reminding her of Brandon sent her irritation meter up even higher.

'I see,' she bit out. 'Sorry,' she added before proceeding over to her desk, where she sat down and turned on the laptop.

Natalie took her time pulling up the page into which she would enter his personal details and requirements, not looking up till she was good and ready.

'So what happens where you *are* working?' she finally asked.

'I sometimes don't show up at all,' he returned.

Charming, she thought.

It seemed men who looked like this were true to type.

Brandon had never been on time for anything. There again, Brandon had had lots of reasons for running late for his dates with her. Or for not showing up at all.

His job as an anti-terrorist agent for one. Plus the wife and two children that she'd never known he had, came the added caustic thought.

She wondered what Mike Stone's excuse was.

'Sounds like you're a workaholic.'

'It's not the first time I've been called that,' he replied with an indifferent shrug.

Natalie liked him less with each passing second. 'Is that why you haven't had much luck finding a wife so far?' she asked rather waspishly.

'No. I could have married any number of women.'

'Really.' Natalie added outrageously arrogant to his rapidly increasing list of flaws.

Finding Mike Stone a wife was going to prove difficult, despite his impressively masculine physique. Her girls all wanted amenable husbands, not up-themselves egotists. Most of them had had unhappy relationships in the past, with difficult and selfish men who hadn't delivered. By the time they came to her, they usually knew exactly what they wanted, and had no intention of settling for anything less.

Natalie suspected that the likes of Mike Stone would not find favour with any of them.

But it wasn't her problem if none of her girls wanted to marry him. She charged her male clients five thousand dollars up front, whether they found a wife at Wives Wanted, or not.

For his money, Mr Stone would be matched and introduced to five very attractive and intelligent women who fitted his criteria the best, and vice versa. After that, it was up to him.

But he'd have to show a bit more charm on a date than he was currently showing if he wanted a wife. Just being sexy was not enough for her once-bitten, twice-shy girls.

Still, that wasn't her problem.

'Since you own a computer software company, Mike,' she said matter-of-factly, 'you'll be familiar with the type of program I use to match up my clients. It's quite basic, really. Mine, however, does have a security check built in, which validates that my clients are exactly who they say they are. I presume you have no objection to that?'

'Nope.'

'Good. Let's get started, then. Your full name.'

'Mike Stone.'

'No, your *full* name,' she said, a touch of exasperation creeping into her voice. 'The name that's on your birth certificate and driving licence.'

'Mike Stone.'

Natalie gritted her teeth. 'Not Michael?'

'Just Mike.'

'Fine. Your address and phone number, please? Mobile as well.'

She typed them in as he rattled them off, thinking to herself that his address of an apartment in Glebe could be good news or bad news. Glebe had become a trendy suburb of late. Its proximity to the inner city and Sydney University was highly valued. But some parts of it were still a bit dumpy.

'Your work address?'

'I work from home.'

Oh-oh. Now that was *definitely* bad news. Okay, so there were some small businesses that were quite successful. But not too many.

'Age,' she said.

'Thirty-four.'

Now *her* eyebrows lifted. She'd thought him older. There was a wealth of life's experience *within* those eyes.

'I'll be thirty-five in December,' he added. 'December the fifteenth.'

'So you're a Sagittarius,' she said as she tapped in that information.

'I don't believe in crap like that.'

'Really.' She should have known. Brandon had said something very similar when she'd claimed the stars deemed them a reasonable match. She was a Virgo, which wasn't a bad match with a Scorpio.

But Natalie wished she'd taken notice of the part that said Scorpio was the sign of dark secrets.

'Marital status?' she went on.

'What?'

'Have you ever been married?'

'Nope.'

'Lots of my clients have been,' she remarked.

'Not me, sweetheart.'

Natalie stiffened before shooting him a wintry glance. 'My name is Natalie,' she said in a voice that would have cut frozen butter. 'Not sweetheart.'

His black eyes glittered for a moment, as though her correction amused him. 'My mistake. Sorry.'

She could see he wasn't. Not at all. But at least she'd made her stand. She couldn't bear men who called women generic names liked sweetheart and honey. It was condescending and demeaning.

'Well, nothing has come back to say that you're not who you say you are,' she told him after a few seconds' wait. Neither was there a warning that he'd ever been arrested, or in prison. 'Now on to your physical description. I can see for myself that your hair is dark brown and very short, and that your eyes are black.'

'They're not black. They're dark brown. They just look black because they're deeply set.'

Deeply set and infuriatingly sexy.

'Right,' she said. 'Height?'

'Six four. Six five, maybe.'

'What's that in centimetres?'

'Lord knows.'

'Never mind. I'll put six five. I'm five ten and you're a good bit taller than me.'

For weight/bodytype, she typed in 'fit and muscly'. She wasn't the only female in the world who liked well-built men.

'Do you smoke?'

'Nope.'

'Do you drink?'

He laughed. 'Do ducks swim?'

'How much do you drink?'

'Depends.'

'On what?'

'On whether I'm working or not. I don't drink when I'm working.'

Natalie sighed. 'And when you're not?'

He shrugged. 'I'm a scotch man. But I like a nice red with evening meals and a cold beer on a hot day.'

'Would you classify yourself as a problem drinker?'

'Certainly not.'

'Hobbies.'

'Hobbies?' he repeated.

'What do you enjoy doing during your leisure hours?' she asked, and looked up from the laptop.

Their eyes met momentarily before his left her face to drift down to where her jacket was straining across her breasts.

'Besides that,' she snapped.

His eyes narrowed on her, and she wondered if he was wondering why she was letting him get under her skin so much.

'I like to work out,' he replied. 'And to go out.'

'Where to?'

'Clubs. Pubs. Wherever I can have a drink with my mates and meet women.'

He'd have no trouble picking up women, Natalie conceded. He wouldn't even have to speak. His hard, sexy body and those hard, sexy eyes would do all the talking for him.

'Are you a good lover?'

The question was out of her mouth before she could stop herself. It was not one of her usual questions. But, thankfully, he didn't know that.

'I've never had any complaints,' came his nonchalant reply.

She almost asked him how much sex he would want from his wife, but she pulled herself up just in time. She'd already overstepped the mark.

'Religion?' she asked instead.

'Nope.'

'An atheist?'

'Nope.'

'What, then?' she asked through gritted teeth.

'The Lord and I haven't had much to do with each other so far, but who knows what the future might hold?'

'Fine. I'll put open-minded on the subject of religion. Education?'

'Not much.'

'Could you be more specific than that?'

'I attended school till I was seventeen, but I didn't sit for my school certificate or my HSC. I've never been to college or university. I'm a self-taught computer genius.'

'*Genius?* My, let's not be too modest here.'

'I'm not being modest. I'm saying it as it is.'

'Fine. But I think I'll enter computer expert. You wouldn't want to put off a potential wife by sounding a little...shall we say...arrogant?'

'I'm not arrogant. I'm honest. But put what you like.'

She intended to. Lord, but he was the most irritating man. 'What's the name of your software company?'

'Stoneware.'

'Stoneware?' She rolled her eyes at him.

'The name amused me,' he said, and actually smiled.

Not a big smile. More a lifting of the corner of his mouth.

'You do have a sense of humour, then?'

'It's not one of my best qualities.'

'Somehow I gathered that,' she muttered. 'Now, Mike, I will understand if you do not want to give me a precise figure, but approximately what is your annual income?'

'I don't mind telling you. Last year Stoneware made six point four million dollars profit. I own seventy per cent of the company, so my share was four point four eight million. I expect this next year to be a much better year, however.'

Natalie swallowed her surprise and said, 'How much better?'

'A *lot* better,' he replied drily. 'We released a couple of new games which have really taken off.'

'I see.'

'I presume that improves my chances of finding a wife?'

His question—and his tone—had a decidedly cynical flavour, which ruffled Natalie's feathers.

'Money alone will not secure you a wife from amongst *my* girls,' she told him crisply.

'Are you sure about that?'

'Quite sure.'

'Pity.'

'What does that mean?'

He stared hard at her, making her squirm on her chair.

'You know, you're not quite what I expected,' was his next, rather cryptic comment, 'but I can see you're still a no-nonsense businesswoman. Like I said, I'm a truthful man. I don't like to con people. I also don't have the time to muck around. The thing is, Ms Fairlane,' he continued as he sat forward on the sofa, his elbows coming to rest on his knees, 'I need a wife before the first week in December.'

# CHAPTER THREE

'THE first week in *December*!' Natalie exclaimed. 'But December's just over a month away!'

'That's right,' Mike said, feeling perversely pleased that he'd got a real rise out of her.

He'd met females like Natalie Fairlane before. For some reason they were sour on life, and on men. That was why they tried to hide their femininity behind masculine-looking clothes. They lived in constant denial of their sex, and their sexuality.

Yet a man would have to be blind not to see that Natalie Fairlane was a looker. With the right make-up and the right outfit, she'd be a knock-'em-dead type. She had all the basic equipment. Gorgeous red hair. Striking blue eyes. A sultry mouth. And, if he was not mistaken, hiding behind that simply awful grey trouser suit was a darned good figure.

'But that's impossible!' she informed him agitatedly. 'It takes a month and a day to get a marriage licence, unless you have a special reason for a special licence. *Do* you?' she demanded to know. 'Oh, this is quite ridiculous. *Why* do you have to be married by then?'

Natalie watched as he sighed, then leant back again, stretching his arms along the back of the sofa, his leather jacket coming apart as he did so.

Natalie did her best not to stare. But, brother, did that man have a chest on him!

'Do you want the long version or the short version?' he said.

'Any version will do,' she told him. 'Provided it makes sense.'

'Fair enough. The thing is, Ms Fairlane, I'm in negotiations with an American company named Comproware who are very interested in a new firewall program I've written. Interested enough to offer me a partnership.'

'And?' Natalie prompted when he stopped talking for a second. Patience was not one of Natalie's virtues.

'Such a partnership would earn my company many millions over the coming years. Unfortunately, the owner of Comproware is a sanctimonious, self-righteous old buzzard named Chuck Helsinger who refuses to go into partnership with any man who isn't married. Married with solid family values, I've been informed.'

'Aah, I'm beginning to see. But why do you call Mr Helsinger self-righteous?'

'He's seventy years old. And his wife is in her forties. His *third* wife.'

'At least he *married* her!'

'Trading your wife in on a younger model every once in a while hardly demonstrates solid family values. Not that I feel all that sorry for any of his wives.

No doubt they only married him in the first place for his money.'

'Which is exactly what you're planning to do,' she pointed out tartly. 'Marrying for Mr Helsinger's money.'

'Right in one, Ms Fairlane. Glad to see you've got the picture.'

'Oh, I've got the picture all right, Mr Stone,' she countered, a furious indignation simmering away inside her. 'Now let me give you *my* picture. If you think I would insult any of my girls by matching a man like you up with any of them, then you can think again. They wouldn't enter into the kind of loveless marriage you're wanting, for all the money in the world. They want real marriages with real husbands and the possibilities of a real family, which I presume wouldn't be on *your* agenda.'

Her tirade didn't seem to have affected him in the slightest. He continued to lounge back in that nonchalantly relaxed pose, his expression as poker-faced as ever.

'You're quite right, Ms Fairlane. I certainly wasn't planning on being a *real* husband. This would be a business arrangement only, with a discreet divorce in the foreseeable future.'

'A business arrangement?' she repeated a bit blankly. 'You mean…no sex?'

'Absolutely no sex.'

Somehow she found that hard to believe. Mike Stone oozed testosterone from every pore.

But then she realised what he meant. Just no sex

with his bought bride. He'd probably still be having it off with other women.

'I'm sorry,' she said stiffly. 'I would still not entertain the thought of putting such an outrageous proposition to any of my girls. It's not what they came to Wives Wanted to get. They would be offended and none would accept.'

'You're quite sure of that?'

'Absolutely.'

'I will pay one million dollars up front. And a further one million if the partnership goes through.'

Natalie gaped before she could stop herself.

'Naturally, I will also cover all expenses associated with the wedding,' the object of her gaping went on before she could regather her composure. 'The marriage will have to look real. Mr Helsinger could be having me investigated.'

'I see,' she said after her mouth finally snapped shut. 'That's a very…generous…offer.'

Generous and tempting.

'It's fair for the amount of work and inconvenience involved. Aside from the bother of going through with a wedding, and making it look the goods, my temporary wife will have to be available to spend a couple of days with me aboard Mr Helsinger's yacht early in December. He's coming here to Sydney to pick up this brand-new luxury boat and look me over at the same time.'

Natalie frowned. 'Yachts don't have huge bedrooms. If you're supposed to be newly-weds, you'll have to share a cabin.'

'I can see the way your mind is working, Ms Fairlane, but I can promise you there won't be any hanky-panky. I don't want to create any problems afterwards. This marriage will not be consummated, so please don't match me up with any female who might fancy herself a *femme fatale*, or who might imagine that I will fall in love with her. I won't,' he finished up with a flash of steel in his hard, dark eyes. 'I don't fall in love and I won't be staying married.'

'You don't have to worry about some poor deluded creature from Wives Wanted trying to seduce you, Mr Stone,' she said, thinking his name reflected his nature. He was made of stone. 'I still have no intention of matching you with *any* of my female clients.'

Natalie would later question why she did what she did next. Was it just for the money, or were there other, darker forces at work?

The money was certainly very tempting. She would be able to pay off her parents' mortgage and give them a lump sum to help with their retirement. Then, when she got the second million—she didn't doubt that the ruthlessly ambitious Mike Stone would get his partnership—she could pay off her own mortgage and maybe go on an overseas holiday. She was getting tired of matching other women to men who actually wanted to marry them. It had once given her a kick to see two of her clients happily wed. Lately, however, a measure of envy had been creeping in.

Despite her disastrous relationship with Brandon, Natalie had always believed she would marry one day. And have a family of her own. When she'd started Wives Wanted three years back, she'd still harboured the hope that one day her Mr Right would walk through the door.

But something had happened to her, post-Brandon. She'd become defensive and aggressive where the opposite sex was concerned. The bottom line was she just didn't trust them.

Men were not attracted to her harder, more cynical persona. She hadn't had a date, or a single lover, since Brandon.

'How about me?' came her curt offer.

*That* got his attention. He sat up straight, his arms falling off the back of the sofa.

*'You?'*

The shock in his voice piqued her considerably.

'Yes, me,' she snapped. 'What's wrong with me?'

What was wrong with her was that he fancied her.

Keeping his hands off the provocative Ms Fairlane might prove difficult, especially on those nights they were thrown together on the yacht. On the other hand, it was clear she wasn't about to help him find a wife from amongst her precious 'girls'.

Suddenly, he understood why. She wanted the job—nope, she wanted the *money*—for herself.

'I suppose you were looking for someone younger,' she said with a flash of those cut-glass blue eyes of hers.

'How old *are* you?' he asked.

'The same age as you. Thirty-four.'

His eyebrows lifted. He would have tagged her as

a couple of years older. But that was probably due to the dreary clothes she was wearing.

'I can look younger,' she said with a proud toss of her head. 'And prettier. If that's what you want.'

'What I want, Ms Fairlane, is a wife who can convince Chuck Helsinger that she's genuinely in love with me. Can you do that?'

Her chin lifted. 'For two million dollars? I'll convince him I adore every single hair on your head.'

Mike smiled as he ran his hand over his very thick crew cut. This, he'd like to see.

His smile faded, however, when he realised he might find it even harder to keep his hands off when Ms Fairlane started playing the besotted bride. He would have to keep reminding himself that she was just doing it for the money.

Damn, but that thought really annoyed him. He hated gold-diggers with a passion.

'I presume you won't entertain any romantic fantasies that I might fall in love with you and want to stay married to you?' he threw at her.

'Don't be ridiculous! You'd be the last man on earth I'd fantasise over.'

'I'm not your type?'

'Only a fool would fantasise over a man who obviously doesn't believe in love and marriage. I am not a fool, Mr Stone,' she finished up firmly.

'In that case, it's a deal, Ms Fairlane.'

Even as he said the words Mike suspected he was going to regret marrying this tough-talking but rather temperamental redhead. But what alternative did he have? Instant wives didn't grow on trees. December would be here before he could blink.

For the first time since they'd met, she suddenly looked uncertain, her hand coming up to her throat in a decidedly vulnerable gesture.

She had a long throat, he noticed. Long and pale, as if she hadn't been out in the sun for ages.

An image popped into Mike's mind of her lying naked on a bed, her whole body pale and soft, her gleaming red hair spread out on the pillow. Her wide eyes would be locked with his, just as they were now, but more so, their expression expectant, yet at the same time excited.

'So…what do we do now?' she said, breaking into his fantasy.

*Why don't I take you to bed?* he wanted to say.

Because that was what he wanted to do. Right now.

It had been too long, Mike realised ruefully, since he'd been to bed with a woman. Richard was right. Celibacy did not sit well with him, not when he was in the company of a woman he fancied.

But there was nothing he could do about it now, certainly not with Ms Fairlane. She'd blow a gasket if he started coming on to her. Nope. He was trapped into a no-sex existence for another couple of months at least. He couldn't even sneak a bit on the side. Cunning old Chuck might find out about it and any partnership would fly out the window.

Just think of the money, he told himself. The same as the mercenary Ms Fairlane is doing. And stop thinking about her being naked, and willing. The odds of her ever being naked and willing with you, Mikey, are about as high as your staying married to her.

Which reminded him. He had a marriage to arrange, and there was no time to lose.

'It's Thursday night,' he returned, glancing at his watch. 'The stores don't close till nine. First, we'll go get a quick bite to eat. After that, I'm taking you engagement-ring shopping.'

# CHAPTER FOUR

'WHAT?' Shock propelled Natalie to her feet. 'Did you say engagement-ring shopping?'

'Absolutely,' Mike replied, rising to his feet also.

'But surely that's not necessary!' She couldn't bear the thought of going into a jewellery shop with him and pretending to be lovers.

'Of course it is,' he returned. 'When I present you to Mr Chuck Helsinger as my wife you're going to have everything my wife should have. That includes a rock on your ring finger and a wardrobe which will knock that dirty old devil's eyes out.'

'But…'

'No buts, please, Natalie. Sorry, but I do have to call you Natalie, since sweetheart and honey and, I presume, darling is out. Unless, of course, you want me to call you Nat.'

She winced at the shortened form of her name, which she'd been called in high school and which she still hated.

'Natalie will be fine,' she bit out.

'Okay. And don't you forget to call me Mike. It wouldn't do for you to address me as Mr Stone.'

'I guess not. Now, about this wardrobe business…'

'Yes?'

'I don't always dress like this, you know. These are just my work clothes.'

'That's a relief.'

Natalie bristled. 'There's no need to insult me.'

'I wasn't insulting you. I was being truthful again. That pant suit you're wearing is simply dreadful. The colour does nothing for you and the cut is far too masculine.'

'I thought you were a computer genius,' she snapped. 'Not the fashion police.'

'I'm a man. And I know what looks good on a woman. The fact that you would even consider buying that outfit in the first place speaks for itself. I'm taking you clothes shopping before December, whether you like it or not.'

'Whatever,' she said, privately conceding that her wardrobe possibly didn't have the clothes necessary for a weekend cruise with the jet set. 'You're paying for it.'

'Good. That's one thing I like about you, Natalie. You know what side your bread is buttered on.'

Natalie tried not to take offence. But it was a bit much, having him criticise her clothes, then tell her that the only thing he liked about her was her mercenary side.

She was tempted to throw at him that the only reason she'd made this appalling deal with him was because of her parents' dire financial position.

Which reminded her.

'I have to make a quick phone call before I leave,' she told him.

'Fine. I'll wait for you out in my car. It's parked just down the street. It's a four-wheel drive. Black, with the number plate STONE. You can't miss it.'

He was gone before she could think of a suitably caustic comment.

Natalie rolled her eyes, then snatched up the phone on the desk. But as she punched in her mother's number she wondered what on earth she was going to tell her.

Nothing, Natalie decided, till the first million was in the bank.

In that case, you'd better stop being so darned prickly, came a sharp warning from her head. Or your would-be benefactor might back out of the deal.

If he wanted to buy her an engagement ring, then fine. If he wanted to buy her a whole wardrobe, that was fine, too. She was not in a position to look this particular gift horse in the mouth.

'It's me again, Mum,' she said when her mother answered. 'Some good news. I've got another client at last.'

'That's good news. Is he rich?'

'Rich enough.'

'Good-looking?'

'Sort of.'

'Do you think you'll be able to find him a wife, more to the point?'

'Yes. No trouble. Which means I'll be flush soon, so don't you go doing anything foolish like pawning things, or borrowing more money from some loan shark. Meanwhile, give me the name of the bank which holds your mortgage.' Her mother always took care of the banking.

She did so, Natalie making a mental note of it as she thought up a strategy to satisfy her parents till she could take care of the whole mortgage. Though Lord knew what she was going to tell them then. Maybe that she'd won the lottery.

'I'll go see the manager tomorrow and organise to have your mortgage refinanced at a lower interest rate,' she offered. 'Rates have come down considerably since you took out that loan. And I'll cover your first few months' payments. Give you some breathing space.'

'Would you? Oh, darling, that would be wonderful. I've been so worried.'

'Yes, Mum, I'm sure you have been. But you don't have to be any longer. I would never see you tossed out of your home. You must know that.'

'You are such a good girl.'

Natalie grimaced. That all depended on one's definition of good. Was it good to marry a man strictly for money?

She supposed it wasn't bad, if the money was for a good cause and you didn't prostitute yourself as well by sleeping with him.

It *was* bad, however, to secretly wish that you were doing just that.

Natalie smothered a groan. It was no use. She had to confess, if only to herself, that just the thought of sleeping with Mike Stone was insidiously exciting.

It was just as well that he was firm on the 'no sex'

part of their arrangement. *And* that he wasn't attracted to her.

Natalie would hate to think what would happen if he fancied her. She would make a fool of herself all right. Not in the way she'd been a fool over Brandon. She would never fall in love with Mike, or think he was anything other than the ruthless, arrogant, mercenary devil that he was.

But she didn't want him lumping her together with all the other silly women he'd obviously bedded and not wedded. In her case, Natalie was determined it was going to be a case of wedded, and not bedded.

'I still can't stay and chat, Mum,' she said. 'I'm going out to dinner with my client.'

'I hope he's paying.'

'Mum, this is me you're talking to. Miss Budgetwise. Of course, he's paying.'

'In that case, eat up, dear. You're getting too thin, you know.'

Natalie had to laugh. Thin, she was not. But her mother always thought she was.

'I'll ring you tomorrow night,' she promised. 'Let you know how I went with the bank. Bye.'

'Bye, dear. And thanks again.'

Natalie resisted the temptation to primp and preen before joining Mike outside. She just grabbed her black carryall, locked the front door and launched herself out into the street.

His car was as macho as he was, she thought as she hurried towards it. An all-black four-wheel drive with darkly tinted windows that exuded a faintly menacing air.

A shiver ran down her spine when the passenger door suddenly swung open, propelled by a black leather-clad arm that disappeared as swiftly as it had appeared.

'You are a most unusual woman,' he said as she climbed in and shut the door behind her.

'In what way?'

'You don't keep a man waiting.'

'Is that a good thing or a bad thing?'

He looked her up and down again. 'That depends.'

'On what?'

'On what we're doing and where we're going.'

'Where *are* we going?'

'This is your turf, Natalie. Where do you suggest we go to get a quick meal?'

'There's a small Italian café a couple of blocks down this street. Bertollini's. They give quick service and serve great pasta and pizza.'

'Sounds just the thing. I'm starving,' he said, and gunned the engine.

'So am I,' she said truthfully.

He shot her a sharp, sidewards glance. 'Don't tell me you're not on a diet. Every female I've ever dated is always on a diet.'

'I never diet.' And she'd never been overweight. She had a high metabolism and a tendency to lose her appetite totally when she was stressed. She'd fallen to a shockingly thin forty-five kilos after Brandon, which had taken her some years to recoup.

But she was fine now, weighing a pleasing fifty-three kilos.

'Stranger and stranger,' he muttered, then said no more till he pulled up outside Bertollini's.

The Italian mamma who owned and ran the café fussed over Natalie in a way she never had before, possibly because she had a man by her side. They were given complimentary glasses of wine and even better service than usual, Natalie feeling embarrassed by the knowing looks all the staff gave her. She had been coming there regularly for three years by herself, so she supposed they thought she'd finally landed herself a boyfriend.

'So how come you're not married yourself?' he asked over their plates of spaghetti Marinara. 'And don't tell me no one has ever asked you,' he added drily. 'You might be a shocking dresser, but you're a good-looking woman.'

Natalie opened her mouth to make some smart crack, then closed it again. If she was going to marry this man—and pretend to adore every hair on his head—then perhaps he should know the truth about her. He claimed to be big on the truth.

'Actually, no one *has* asked me,' she admitted. 'I spent the best years of my life on a man whom I hoped would ask me one day. But he never did. I found out why after four years of loving him, and making endless excuses for him.'

'Don't tell me,' Mike said drily. 'Let me guess. He was already married.'

'How did you know?'

'Sweetheart, it's written all over you. Oops, sorry. That just slipped out.'

'What do you mean, it's written all over me?' she demanded to know.

'For Pete's sake, just look at you.'

'There's nothing wrong with me!'

'There's everything wrong with you. If you still want to get married for real. And I suppose you do. Most females do, for some reason. Then it's just as well I came along.'

'Meaning?' she said stiffly.

'You need someone to tell you as it is, woman. And to sex you up at bit.'

'Sex me up?' she choked out, glad that no one was standing near their table at that moment.

'Yep. You're never going to catch a guy looking and acting like you do, Natalie. They might give you a bit occasionally, but they won't stay the night, and they sure as hell won't ask you to marry them.'

Natalie was torn between asking him if he'd give her a bit and telling him to shut his appallingly insensitive mouth.

'You're an expert on the subject, are you?' she said tartly.

'Yep.'

'My, aren't I the lucky one!'

His eyes narrowed thoughtfully on her across the table as he forked some spaghetti into his mouth and chewed it slowly. At last, he put down the fork and picked up his glass of Chianti.

'I'm often told that I'm far too blunt,' he said after

he took a decent swallow of the wine. 'But sometimes you have to be cruel to be kind. Would you rather I lie to you?'

There was an oddly touching sincerity in his words, and his face. Clearly, he hadn't meant to offend her, even though he had.

Natalie could do one of two things. Go back to prickly, or embrace his advice. In truth, she did still want to get married. And have a family. Especially have a family.

The thought that she might never have a child was too depressing for words. And whilst she'd known for some time that her lack of success with the opposite sex was entirely her own fault, perhaps it needed a man like Mike to make her face her off-putting ways. And to make her try to change them.

She couldn't successfully carry off the role of his besotted new bride, dressing and acting as she had been. Why not use this opportunity to try to become a different woman? A softer, sexier, less aggressive woman.

She sucked in a deep breath and let it out slowly. 'I'm well aware that I've fallen into some bad habits. I never used to be this hard and cynical. But when I found out Brandon not only had a wife, but two children as well, I totally lost it.'

'How did he get away with it?' Mike asked. 'I mean, how did he hide a wife and two children from you for…how long was it?'

'Four years.'

'Bloody hell. That's a long time. Surely you must have suspected something.'

'I should have, but I didn't. His work gave him the perfect excuse for when he had to go away, and when he couldn't tell me where he was going, or why I couldn't contact him. He was a spy, you see.'

'A spy!' Mike exclaimed. 'Lord, Natalie, you didn't fall for that old chestnut, did you?'

'He was—*is*—a spy,' she ground out firmly. 'He works for ASIO in their anti-terrorist unit. I know this for a fact, Mike. I was working in a government position myself at the time.'

'What as?'

'I was personal assistant to one of the ministers in the Premier's Department. I took six months long service leave after the fiasco with Brandon. And I never went back. I started up Wives Wanted instead.'

'Why?'

'Why?'

'Yes, why? No lies now. Give it to me straight.'

'I guess there were lots of reasons. A few weeks into my long service leave, I started looking up introduction agencies on the internet. I was only thirty, after all. And terribly lonely. But after some simply awful email experiences with men who just wanted to get into my pants, I decided to start up an agency of my own, one which fulfilled my own requirements for a husband. I soon discovered there were lots of other women out there like me, and lots of men too who'd been burned, but still wanted wives and children.'

'Makes you sound like a do-gooder. Admit it, Natalie. You started Wives Wanted to find *yourself* a husband.'

She sighed. 'I suppose so. Unfortunately, it didn't work out that way. But it still satisfied something in me to see women get what they wanted where men were concerned. I guess it was a form of revenge and therapy rolled into one.'

'Yeah, I can understand that.'

'What about you?' she asked, sick of talking about herself. And going over such painful old ground.

'What about me?'

'What made you so sour on love and marriage?'

'I'm not sour on love and marriage. Good luck to those who find happiness in both, I say. They're just not for me.'

'But why? And don't lie to me. Tell me the truth, like you say you always do.'

The muscles in his jaw stiffened, then twitched.

'There are some truths better left unsaid,' he muttered, and returned to his meal.

Natalie stared at him, unrequited curiosity destroying her own appetite. 'That's it? You're not going to tell me?'

He never said a word till he finished his food. 'Nope,' he said as he put down his fork.

'Well, thank you very much,' she snapped.

'You don't need to know all the ins and outs of my life. It's not as though we're getting married for real.'

'I told you mine,' she threw at him.

'Women like to talk about themselves,' he said brusquely. 'Men don't.'

Natalie's frustration level zoomed up to maximum. She couldn't stand men who did this to her. It reminded her too much of Brandon, who'd been the sneakiest, most manipulative bastard in the world, worming every single detail of her life out of her, then telling her virtually nothing about his own life.

If and when Natalie ever married, it would be to a man who kept nothing from her, who told her everything that was in his head, and in his heart. He would trust her with his secrets, and his soul. He would never play her for a fool in any way, shape or form. Because love wasn't cruel. It was kind, and tender, and sensitive.

Natalie stared at the man sitting across the table from her and realised he was incapable of being kind, and tender, and sensitive. His so-called truthfulness was nothing more than ill-disguised rudeness. He disliked and disrespected women for some reason. And had no intention of telling her why.

She'd made a deal with the devil agreeing to this marriage. But there was no backing out now.

Still, she didn't have to do what she didn't want to do.

'I'm already well aware that men don't like to talk,' she told him coldly. 'Which is a pity. It might do them some good. Women, on the other hand, don't like being made to look foolish, so I won't be coming engagement-ring shopping with you tonight. I know I will have to pretend devotion in front of Mr

Helsinger. I won't, however, pretend in front of some simpering salesgirl. My grandmother willed me all her jewellery. I will wear her engagement ring. *And* her wedding ring, when the time comes. Take it or leave it.'

Again, he just shrugged, his indifference annoying Natalie considerably. 'Whatever. Provided they're nice rings. Not cheap ones. A man in my position would not buy cheap rings for his wife.'

'They are beautiful rings,' Natalie ground out through gritted teeth.

'In that case, good. It saves time and trouble. But I won't back down on the clothes issue. Still, that can wait till a later date. Getting that marriage licence, however, can't wait. You said it takes a month. Where do you go to get it?'

'The registry office. In the city. You'll need to take your birth certificate with you. I presume you have a copy.'

'Nope.'

'You'll have to get one, then, won't you? If you go into the department of Births, Deaths and Marriages personally, you can pick it up over the counter. That's in the city, too.'

'Good. We can get it all done first thing tomorrow morning. I'll pick you up at nine.'

Natalie bristled. 'You might like to ask if I'm busy tomorrow morning.'

'Are you?'

'I have a hairdressing appointment. I go every Friday morning.' It was an indulgence, she knew. But it was the most relaxing thing she did all week. Natalie especially enjoyed the head massage after the shampoo.

His eyes lifted to her hair. 'In that case I suggest you dump your present hairdresser before December and find someone with a bit more pizzazz.'

Natalie glared at him across the table. 'And I suggest *you* find someone else to marry.'

He seemed startled, as though he wasn't aware that he was being abominably tactless. 'You *like* the way your hair looks?'

'*I* did my hair this way today. Not my hairdresser.'

'Oh, I see. So you *deliberately* make yourself look as unattractive as possible whenever you're interviewing a new male client.'

*Did* she? Perhaps. She had a tendency to be self-destructive when depressed. And she'd been depressed with her personal life for several months.

'What time will you be finished at the hairdresser's?' he asked abruptly.

'Around twelve.'

'I'll pick you up at your place at one-thirty.'

'Fine. I'll be ready.'

'Good. That's it for tonight, then,' he said, and called for the bill.

He left a hefty tip, Natalie noticed.

Brandon had been a big tipper. He'd been a big man, too. There were lots of similarities between the two men, Natalie realised. Too many for comfort.

When he slid the four-wheel drive into the kerb outside her house, she refused to let him get out of his car and walk her to the door. She didn't want to stand next to him on her doorstep, dying to ask him to come in, hating herself for already feeling excited about tomorrow.

She didn't like him. But she was wildly attracted to him. Just sitting next to him in that car for less than three minutes had rendered her breathless.

She could feel his eyes still on her as she unlocked her door. He'd said he wouldn't move off till she was safely inside.

That reminded her of Brandon also, the way Mike's male presence made her feel protected. Was it just because of his size, and his strength? Whatever, being around Mike Stone gave her that same slightly help-less and very feminine feeling that was as irritating as it was seductive.

Natalie hated the fragility of that feeling. And the frustration it inevitably evoked.

At the same time, she suspected that come one-thirty tomorrow she would open this same door look-ing totally different from the way she looked at this moment. If nothing else, Natalie would have the sat-isfaction of seeing those hard, dark eyes widen with surprise.

Not that it would change anything. Mike still wouldn't like her. And she wouldn't like him.

But sexual attraction wasn't always about liking, Natalie was not totally surprised to discover. Nor was it linked to common sense. It had a mind of its own. A powerful and primitive mind, which didn't listen to logic; which was compelled by base and basic instincts; which reduced a woman to little more than an empty vessel, aching to be filled.

Natalie lay in bed later that night aching to be filled by Mike Stone.

'What a fool I am,' she muttered to herself as she tossed and turned.

But the fierceness of her physical frustration served the purpose of changing her mind about the following day. She would not wear grey, but neither would she doll herself up for this man. Her pride would not let her, regardless of what her ego—or her treacherous body—wanted.

Such a transformation could backfire on her, anyway. Mike might look at her very askance, perhaps jumping to the wrong conclusion. He might think she was a closet *femme fatale*, with designs on making him fall for her and stay married to her.

If he thought that, he'd run a mile.

To risk losing two million dollars for the sake of a moment's triumph was ridiculous. If she had some chance of actually seducing the man, it might have been worth it. But Mike had been very adamant on the score of the 'no sex' clause in their contract.

Which reminded her. Perhaps she should make him actually sign a contract. After all, what guarantee did she have that he would give her the two million? A man like him wouldn't care if he ever got a legal divorce. Remarrying didn't interest him. He might just walk away when he got his partnership and give her nothing.

On the other hand, he wouldn't want a nasty legal

fight on his hands. Or bad publicity. From the sounds of things, Chuck Helsinger wouldn't be impressed.

Still, she would be stupid if she didn't bring the subject up. Yes, that was how she had to continue dealing with Mike. In a very practical and pragmatic fashion. None of that silly, soft female stuff.

Now if she could only get to sleep...

But Natalie found it very difficult to sleep. She didn't drop off till well after two, and then it was to dream of a faceless man whom she allowed to use her body in the most shameless fashion. He turned her this way and that, taking her repeatedly, making her cry out with the darkest of possessions. The dreams—and the ravagement—seemed to go on for hours. Then, when she was totally spent, he began to walk away, without a word.

But at the last moment he glanced over his shoulder, and she saw his eyes. They were deeply set, and dark, and horribly hard.

'Mike,' she called out in her dream.

But he just kept on walking.

# CHAPTER FIVE

MIKE smiled wryly to himself as he drove towards Natalie's place the next day.

Richard's response when Mike had called this morning to tell his friend whom he'd secured for his wife still amused him.

'You're joshing me!' Richard had exclaimed. 'Natalie Fairlane! Madame Tough-nut herself?'

A very funny but apt description in Mike's opinion.

Richard's initial surprise had quickly subsided once Mike had explained the lucrative terms he'd offered the owner of Wives Wanted.

'Amazing what some women will do for money,' Richard had remarked in a cynical tone that echoed Mike's opinion.

Still, there was no doubt she would impress old Helsinger, once he got her wearing some decent clothes. Natalie couldn't have *always* dressed as she'd been dressed yesterday. She'd had a lover for four years. Married guys who had women on the side went for sexy pieces of skirt, not uptight, women's-lib types who hid their female assets behind unflattering gear.

Mike couldn't wait to re-uncover Natalie's female assets. He'd glimpsed a more-than-adequate bust stretching that awful grey jacket. And she was tall enough to have good legs. He'd noted slim ankles when she'd sat down at the café and crossed her legs.

Pity about her shoes, though. Black pumps with thick heels didn't do a thing for any woman. Nor did grim grey trouser suits.

He'd love to see her in tight hipster jeans that hugged her body and left absolutely nothing to the imagination. He'd team them with a sexy top and some come-to-bed stilettos.

The sudden awareness of a hard-on reminded Mike that this was not a sensible train of thought at this moment, muttering a steely reproof at his wayward flesh as he slid his car into the kerb outside Natalie's place.

It was a terraced house, one in a long line of identical houses that stretched down her street. The only difference between them was the paintwork.

Some of the others were a bit on the garish side, but Natalie's was painted in traditional federation colours. Cream walls, with forest-green roof and ironwork, and a splash of burgundy here and there. The front door and window sill were burgundy, plus the guttering. The tiny front yard was totally paved in old-fashioned terracotta tiles, with green glazed pots filled with palms sitting in each corner.

Mike stayed where he was for a further five minutes before climbing out from behind the wheel and making his way slowly to her door, before finally ringing the brass bell.

'You're late,' she snapped as she swept open the door.

'I don't consider five minutes late,' he retorted, thinking all the while that the improvement in her appearance was only minimal.

She was still wearing trousers, this time a black linen pair, topped by a crisp cream shirt that resembled a schoolgirl's blouse. Her hair was somewhat schoolgirlish as well, tied at the nape of her neck with a black ribbon.

Mike did not have a schoolgirl fetish. He liked his women to look like women.

Only her face got his approval. She seemed to have taken some trouble there, make-up making her big blue eyes look bigger and bluer, and her full mouth look...

Better not look at her mouth, he told himself sternly. Lush lips enhanced with scarlet lipstick did wicked things to him at the best of times.

Her perfume was on the seductive side as well.

'Shall we get going, then?' he said abruptly.

'I'll just get my bag and jacket.'

'You won't need a jacket. It's twenty-eight degrees.'

She set decidedly cool eyes on him, making him wish he'd brought *his* jacket.

'I always take a jacket with me. You never know in Sydney when a southerly change is going to sweep in.'

'Fine,' he said, with a nonchalant shrug.

'Are you always this impatient?' he grumbled when she returned with a black handbag.

*     *     *

No, Natalie wanted to confess, shame and self-disgust bringing a guilty colour to her face. Only when I've been sitting there for the last fifteen minutes like a cat on a hot tin roof, forcing myself not to run to the front window with every passing car. Telling myself I was crazy to feel like this over a man who wanted nothing from me but an act. Hating myself for feeling physically sick when one-thirty came and you hadn't arrived.

'I guess I'm a bit nervous,' she bit out by way of an excuse. 'It's not every day that I agree to marry a man I hardly know.'

'Not having second thoughts, are you?' he asked.

Natalie suppressed a shiver as her gaze swept over him. She'd found him attractive in blue jeans and leather jacket yesterday. Today, she found him devastating.

Was it her dream of last night that had heightened her hunger for him? Or was it the tight black jeans and equally tight black T-shirt that made her crave to touch his magnificent body?

Nothing was hidden from her eyes today. She could see it all, from his broad shoulders and incredible biceps down to his flat stomach and slim hips.

Natalie worked out at a gym herself three times a week and was used to seeing good male bodies. But Mike's was something else.

He made Brandon look like a weakling, which he hadn't been. He'd been very fit and toned.

'No,' she said. 'Your being a friend of Richard Crawford's is an excellent reference. He's a very reputable man. But I got to thinking last night and I want a pre-nuptial agreement which guarantees what you promised me.'

If she was worried that he might react negatively to her request, then she shouldn't have.

'Fair enough,' he said with one of his now-familiar shrugs.

'You agree?'

'Absolutely. Money matters are best not left up to chance. I'll have Rich line up a meeting with his legal team at the bank. They can organise a pre-nup which stipulates the terms I outlined.'

Mike's mentioning the word bank brought a gasp to her lips. 'Oh, Lord, I forgot.'

'Forgot what?'

'I promised to do a job for my parents today at their bank. They're having some money problems,' she added, then wished she hadn't. 'It clean went out of my mind.'

'So where is their bank? I can drive you there after we're finished.'

'Would you? It's not in the city. It's in Parramatta.'

'No trouble. It won't take for ever to do the marriage licence bit. Not if we get moving.'

Natalie was rather relieved to get moving, till Mike climbed up into his black vehicle next to her and shut the door after him. Once again, the enclosed space combined with Mike's overwhelming maleness quickened her breathing, making her regret the foolishness of asking him to drive her to Parramatta.

Whatever had possessed her?

Silly question. The answer was sitting right next to her with all his disturbing machismo.

Natalie drew in a deep breath, then let it out slowly, telling herself it wasn't a crime to look, even to lust. Men did it all the time. The crime would be to let Mike know how he affected her.

She was very glad now that she'd dressed sensibly today. She would have despised herself if she'd tried to make herself into a *femme fatale*.

As it turned out, fate—and Friday afternoon—let her off the hook where any trip to Parramatta was concerned. Parking problems plus long queues meant it was four by the time they'd secured Mike's birth certificate, and then their marriage licence.

'It's too late to go to Parramatta now,' she said as they left the registry office.

'Is this problem of your parents' urgent?' Mike asked. 'Can it wait till Monday?'

'It'll have to, I suppose,' she replied, not happy with herself for having forgotten to fulfil her promise.

'What is the problem, exactly?' Mike asked as they walked together back towards the parking station.

Natalie bit her bottom lip. She knew it had been a mistake to mention that. The last thing she wanted was for Mike to know why she was marrying him. Telling him some sob story about her doing it for a noble cause would sound so lame now. And so Hollywood.

Far better Mike continue to think she wanted his money for herself. No way did she want his pity. Pity was the last thing she wanted from him, she thought with perverse amusement.

At the same time, she had to come up with some plausible explanation. Mike was no fool.

'Dad's got behind with the mortgage a bit. But if they refinance their loan at the current rate—which is much lower than when they took it out—they should be able to manage better.'

'You sound like you know what you're talking about. Are you an accountant?'

'Not certified. But I have a business degree.'

'I thought you said you were a secretary.'

'I was a personal assistant, not a secretary.'

Mike suddenly took hold of her arm and pulled her to a halt. 'Rich's bank refinances loans. He'll help you out if I ask him to. He owes me a favour.'

'How's that?'

'He owns shares in Stoneware.'

'Ah-h-h.'

'So now you know my secret,' he said with a wry smile. 'I'm not just marrying you to get Helsinger's money for myself. I have other, less selfish motives.'

'We all have more than one motive for what we do,' she replied, thinking of her parents again.

'That sounded deep. So what are *your* other motives for marrying me?'

'Oh, no, you're not going to do that to me again.'

'Do what?'

'Make me reveal all my personal secrets, then tell me absolutely nothing about yourself. We both know the main reason why this marriage is going to happen.

The bottom line is money. That's all you have to know, Mike Stone.'

His dark eyes actually twinkled at her, making his face look softer for a moment. 'Fair enough. Look, Rich's bank is just around the corner from here. Come on. He'll still be in his office, being the workaholic that he is.'

Natalie found herself being propelled back along the pavement at considerable speed, giving her a glimpse of Mike's physical strength.

'But we can't just barge in there!' she protested breathlessly as they dodged people going the other way.

'Besides, isn't his bank a merchant bank? They wouldn't handle home mortgages.'

'He'll do it for me.'

'But—'

'For pity's sake, woman, let me help you out here. Or does letting a man help you out go against your women's lib creed?'

That silenced her. Because she'd never thought of herself as a women's libber. And she didn't like the tag one bit.

'That's better,' he muttered as he ushered her silent self into a solid grey-stone building that looked old enough to have been built by convicts.

Inside, however, the décor of the foyer was spacious and plush, exuding the sort of rich yet sombre atmosphere Natalie associated with Swiss banks.

Mike steered her past the security guards who flanked the lifts, actually saying, 'Hi,' to them as if he was an old friend. They were soon exiting on the fifth floor, Natalie's shoes sinking into thick red carpet as they walked along a wide corridor dotted with heavy wooden doors. The one right at the end had a gold plate with Richard Crawford's name on it, plus CEO underneath.

By the time Mike reached for the knob on this door, Natalie's agitation had increased considerably. This was going to be so embarrassing. And awkward. How was she going to keep her parents' dire financial situation from Mike if he accompanied her into his friend's office?

Which he would.

The first door opened, not into Richard Crawford's office, but his secretary's.

'Hello, Pattie,' Mike said to the middle-aged brunette who was busy tapping away on her computer. 'Is the boss in?'

'Where else?' she replied with a dry glance. 'Do me a favour, Mike, and take him out somewhere for a drink, would you? I have visitors coming tonight and need to get home before dark.'

'Will do, sweetheart,' Mike said.

Natalie rolled her eyes at his calling the woman sweetheart. Still, at least he was consistent.

'Aren't you going to introduce us?' the secretary asked with a quick smile towards Natalie.

'Sorry. Forgot my manners. Natalie, this is Pattie Woodward. Pattie, this is Natalie Fairlane,' he said. 'My fiancée.'

Natalie was glad she smothered her gasp in time.

'Thought I'd pop in and tell Rich the good news,' Mike rattled on whilst the secretary just stared at Natalie.

Natalie wondered if Pattie's shock was due to Mike getting married at all, or the woman he'd chosen to marry. Clearly, she wasn't his usual type.

'Well!' Pattie exclaimed at last. 'Congratulations to you both. And when's the wedding to be?'

'As soon as possible,' Mike replied. 'And, no, it's not a shotgun wedding. We just can't wait to be man and wife,' he added, shocking Natalie when he snaked one of his arms around her waist and pulled her hard against him. 'Isn't that right, darlin'?' he added, his large fingertips rubbing along her ribcage just under her right breast.

This time she did gasp, her heart fluttering in her chest as her nipples tightened in the most exquisitely pleasurable way. Without thinking, she lifted her eyes to his, her lips parting to say 'yes' in the most horribly breathless fashion.

His eyes narrowed before dropping to her still-parted lips, Natalie's heart lurching when he swung her round and his head began to descend.

My God! He was going to kiss her. Right here. In front of Pattie.

And she was going to let him.

# CHAPTER SIX

'Ahem!'

Mike whirled round to see Richard standing in the open doorway of his office, giving him the sternest of looks.

Mike supposed he should have been grateful that his friend had stopped him from kissing Natalie.

But, damn it all, she'd felt so good in his arms. A few more seconds and he'd have found out what she tasted like. And what she kissed like.

Now he'd never know.

'Hi there, Rich,' he said, frustration still fizzing along his veins. 'Guess what? Natalie and I are engaged. Thought we'd come and tell you the good news personally.'

Richard, who looked his usual banker self in a navy pinstriped suit, didn't turn a hair. 'Really. How nice. My congratulations to you both. We'll have to have a celebratory drink together. You can have an early mark, Pattie.'

'I won't say no to that,' his secretary replied with a quick smile and some instant bustle. 'Thanks, boss.'

'My pleasure. Come on inside for a sec, you two. I have a few things to finish up before we can leave.'

As Mike pushed her ahead of him into Richard Crawford's office Natalie was wishing that the floor would open up and swallow her. She knew her face was still burning. And so were her nipples.

What would have happened if Richard hadn't interrupted them?

The prospect didn't bear thinking about.

Thankfully, Mike steered her over to a chair before pulling one up for himself. She really needed some breathing space from him. He was still fairly close, but not as close as he'd been out there in front of Pattie's desk.

Natalie sucked in some deep breaths whilst Richard closed the office door and walked round to sit behind his own impressive desk.

The whole office was impressive, Natalie finally had the presence of mind to notice. And the view through the window behind Richard's desk was second to none, overlooking Hyde Park and the Botanical Gardens.

'Did you have a reason for telling Pattie that you and Natalie were engaged?' Richard said straight away. 'I thought you would both want to keep your marriage confidential.'

Natalie couldn't have agreed with Richard more. She glanced over at Mike for his explanation.

He seemed annoyingly unperturbed by everything. 'If Helsinger is having me investigated, I thought it best that everyone—other than my closest friends, of course—thinks this is a genuine love match.'

'I see,' Richard said. 'So you and Natalie were just pretending out there.'

'Of course.'

Natalie just stopped herself from staring over at him. Because what she'd felt pressing into her stomach hadn't felt like pretence.

Richard turned his businesslike gaze on her. 'Natalie? You don't mind pretending you're in love with Mike?'

'Only when it's necessary,' she replied, pleased that she sounded nicely composed.

'Which it will be when we're on the yacht with the Helsingers,' Mike pointed out. 'So we need a bit of practice beforehand. By the way, Natalie wants a proper pre-nup.'

Richard nodded. 'Sensible of her.'

'Could you have one drawn up for us both to sign?' Mike went on, leaving Natalie trying to look suitably sensible and pragmatic about everything.

'I can.'

'The first million is to be paid into her account on the day of our wedding. The second when the partnership becomes a reality.'

'Fine,' Richard returned. 'So when will this wedding be?'

'Just over a month from today is the earliest it can be,' Mike said. 'Isn't that right, Natalie?'

'Yes. You need a special licence to make it any earlier. But that might look suspicious.'

Richard began flipping over his desk calendar. 'Today's the twenty-eighth of October,' he said. 'The third of December is a Saturday.'

'The third of December it will be, then,' Mike said.

Richard frowned. 'That's cutting it pretty fine. Didn't you say Helsinger arrives in Sydney on the fourth?'

'Yep.'

'When do you have to join him and his wife on the yacht?'

'From the fifth till the seventh.'

'Given you'll only have been married two days by then, you'll have to act like newly-weds.'

Natalie grimaced. How on earth was she going to endure pretending to be Mike's blushing bride?

'Just think of the money,' Mike said with a glance at her face.

'Just look like you two did out in Pattie's office a few minutes ago,' Richard said drily, 'and you'll convince the devil himself that you're madly in love. Now, are you planning on a church wedding?'

'No,' Natalie jumped in. 'I wouldn't like that.' She would not mock God with such a scandalous marriage.

'A celebrant, then,' Richard suggested. 'You could use my penthouse for the ceremony. Holly and I have moved into our new house, but we've kept the penthouse as a getaway. It would make a nice setting for a wedding.'

Natalie remembered that when Richard Crawford had signed up with Wives Wanted, his address had been a new swish apartment in East Balmain.

'You could stay there together till you have to board Helsinger's yacht,' Richard offered.

'We won't say no to that,' Mike said. 'Much better

than a hotel where we'd be on show all the time. Thanks, Rich.'

'Yes, thank you, Richard,' Natalie concurred. *Much* better than staying in some honeymoon suite at a city hotel. That could have been awkward, and seriously embarrassing. Richard's penthouse was sure to have more than one bedroom.

'I'll ring Reece and get the number of that celebrant he and Alanna used,' Mike went on.

Natalie blinked, then swivelled to face Mike. 'Are you talking about the Diamonds?'

'Yep. The one and the same couple you brought together. They're close friends of mine.'

Natalie could not have been more astounded. 'Good heavens!'

'Why so surprised?'

'They…er…just don't seem like your type of people.'

Reece Diamond was a property tycoon, with more looks and charisma than any man had a right to. He was famous for throwing glamorous parties where the women wore designer gowns and the guests were served caviare and champagne.

She couldn't imagine Mike mixing in that crowd.

'I met Reece through my dealings with Rich here,' he explained. 'He lent us both money when we needed it. The three of us have been friends ever since.'

Natalie actually knew Reece and Alanna better than most of her clients. She'd been genuinely happy when their rather pragmatic marriage had blossomed into a true love match.

'Alanna hasn't had any recurrence of that memory loss she had a while back, has she?' she asked, regretting that she hadn't kept in touch since Alanna's accident.

'Nope,' Mike said. 'She's fine. They're having a baby, did you know? So is Holly. Rich's wife.'

'How lovely for you,' Natalie managed to say, even whilst a huge wave of depression swamped her.

Everyone she knew seemed to be having babies. One of her old girlfriends from work had rung her this week to say that she and her husband were expecting. Her hairdresser had regaled her with similar news this morning.

Babies, babies everywhere. But not for her.

Well, certainly not till you stop wasting your time on the Mr Wrongs of this world, she lectured herself.

Still, her marriage to Mike wasn't going to last for too long. There was still time for her to find Mr Right, she decided with a return to more positive thinking.

'Actually, the main reason we popped in to see you, Rich,' Mike continued, 'was because Natalie's parents have a problem meeting their mortgage. She was going to go to their bank today about refinancing, but we ran out of time. I suggested you might be able to help her out.'

'Be glad to. I presume they've run into arrears?'

'Somewhat.'

'Is their bank threatening to repossess?'

'Yes,' she admitted reluctantly.

'Why didn't you tell me things were as bad as that?' Mike demanded to know.

She turned a cool face towards him. 'It wasn't any of your business.'

'It is if this is the reason you agreed to marry me.'

'What does it matter why I agreed to marry you? The end result will be the same. You will hopefully get your partnership and I will get two million dollars. What I do with it should not concern you, just as what you do with your money doesn't concern me.'

'She's right, Mike,' Richard said matter-of-factly.

Yes, she was, Mike appreciated. But that didn't make any of it more palatable. He much preferred thinking of her as a tough-talking, mercenary creature, not some sweet, self-sacrificing daughter.

Still, he supposed two million dollars was a lot more than what was owed on that mortgage. She would still reap in a considerable sum for herself. That still made her reasonably mercenary.

'Okay,' he said. 'I won't quibble. Can you arrange some refinancing, Rich?'

'Not right away. But if Natalie comes in to see me on Monday morning with all the particulars and a letter of authority from her parents, then I can make sure their home is safe till she can pay off the mortgage in total. Will that be satisfactory to you, Natalie?'

'Perfectly. Thank you, Richard. This is very good of you.'

'I'm glad to be of help. On principle, I hate it when

banks start threatening to repossess. There is always another way. What time would you like to come in Monday morning. Ten suit you?'

'Ten is fine. My time's my own on the whole.'

'Good. You can both sign the pre-nup at the same time. Now are we still going to have that celebratory drink? I can't stay too long. I want to get home to Holly.'

'I'm sorry,' Natalie jumped in, 'but I can't. I have to be getting home myself. I have things I have to do.'

'What things?' Mike asked in the lift on the way down.

'Female things.'

Like what? Mike thought irritably. Wash her hair? Paint her toenails? Shave her legs?

His mind suddenly filled with the image of her lying back naked in a bath with one bare leg propped up provocatively on the side whilst she ran a razor in long, languid strokes from her ankle to her knee, then up her thighs.

The lift doors opening broke into his fantasy, startling him. For Mike was not a man given to such fantasies. When he thought of sex, it was in more basic terms.

Natalie, however, seemed to be inspiring him to think in more seductive scenarios.

Was it just the challenge her prickly self presented?

Probably. He never could resist a challenge.

But he aimed to this time. No way was he going to risk rejection, or spoiling the deal of a lifetime. His male hormones would just have to behave themselves for a while.

'You don't have to drive me home,' Natalie announced snippily as she stepped out of the lift. 'I can just as easily catch a taxi.'

He looked at her hard, then shook his head. Damn, but she was an annoying woman. He was constantly torn between wanting to seduce her, and strangle her.

'Don't be ridiculous,' he ground out, taking her by the elbow and urging her across the foyer. 'I might not quite be in Rich's mould, but I'm gentleman enough to know that when you take a lady somewhere, you take her home afterwards.'

# CHAPTER SEVEN

NATALIE could not wait to get out of Mike's car. This time, however, he insisted on walking her to the door.

'What are you going to tell your parents?' he asked whilst she fumbled for her house keys.

'I have no idea,' she muttered, sighing her frustration when she dropped the darn things. 'Maybe I'll say I won the Lotto,' she said as she bent to pick them up.

But Mike swooped up the keys just before her, their faces staying level for a long moment, his dark eyes boring into hers.

'You should tell them the truth.'

His penetrating gaze kept hers prisoner as they both rose to their feet, her keys still in his hands.

'You have to be kidding,' she said. 'My mother would have a pink fit.'

Actually, Natalie wasn't too sure about that. Her mother had probably reached the stage where she'd be happy with the role of mother of the bride under any circumstances. She was always bemoaning the fact that her daughter could find rich husbands for other girls but not herself.

'My father wouldn't like it, either,' she added.

'I'm sure both your parents would be supportive,

once you explained the situation. They're going to benefit substantially, after all.'

'There's more to life than money,' she snapped.

'Only when you have it,' he countered just as sharply, making her wonder what hardships he'd once encountered in his life.

'With your parents in on everything,' Mike argued, 'our marriage would be even more convincing. We could have proper family photos taken to show Helsinger.'

Natalie winced. 'But that would mean a proper wedding dress.'

'You were always going to have that.'

'*Was* I?'

'Absolutely. And a proper honeymoon wardrobe.'

His eyes ran down her black trousers, right down to her black pumps, then back up again, his expression disapproving. No, worse than disapproving, Natalie conceded. Closer to disgusted.

'You have a great figure, Natalie. Why do you hide it?'

She stiffened. 'I don't hide it.'

'Yeah, you do. And I think I know why. You're scared.'

'Scared of what?'

'Of some man wanting you and using you again.'

'My! A pop psychologist as well as a fashion expert and a computer genius!' she scoffed, even whilst she knew he was dead right.

He stared at her with hard, unfathomable eyes,

making her long to know what he was thinking. Probably that she was a total bitch.

But that was all right. She wanted him to think that, didn't she? Because right at this moment she was afraid of *him*, afraid of what he could make her feel and want, afraid of what might happen if she abandoned her defences and started dressing as she had once dressed for Brandon.

'Could I have my keys, please?' she asked with prim politeness.

He stared at her some more before finally dropping them into the palm of her outstretched hand. Then, before she could stop him, he reached out and picked up a long strand of hair that had come loose earlier.

She stiffened as he fingered it, her skin breaking out into goose-bumps when he slowly looped it behind her ear.

'How long is it, I wonder,' he said in a low, husky voice, 'since you really let your hair down?'

Natalie's head whirled at the thought of doing just that. With him.

Their eyes met, and held.

'Have a good weekend,' he said abruptly, then turned on his heels. 'I'll see you Monday morning,' he threw over his shoulder as he strode towards the front gate.

'Oh, and Natalie…' He turned back again at the gate. 'Start wearing your grandmother's engagement ring.'

She clenched her teeth and sucked in some much-needed air. 'Anything else?' she bit out.

He looked her up and down again. 'Some new clothes wouldn't go astray. But I guess that can wait till I take you shopping. I don't trust your taste. Now off you go and do your female things. I have some *male* things I have to do. See you.'

Natalie found herself gripping her keys with white-knuckled intensity. What kind of male things?

But deep in her heart of hearts she knew, didn't she?

He was going to have sex, with one of those many females he could have married, but hadn't. He would probably spend the whole night with her—maybe the whole weekend—making love in all sorts of ways.

By the time Natalie managed to insert her key into the deadlock and let herself inside, a dark and self-destructive jealousy had taken possession of her. The temptation to do anything to spoil Mike's plans for a sex-filled weekend almost extended to telling her parents the truth.

Because she knew how they'd react.

Her mother would be consumed with curiosity and her father with worry. They would both demand to meet this man who planned to marry their daughter, but not stay married to her. The money angle might sway total objection up front, but they would still want to look Mike over before letting their precious child put pen to paper and sell herself like that.

Which was only sensible, of course. There were a lot of weirdos in this world. And whilst Natalie didn't think for one moment that Mike was a weirdo—just a ruthlessly ambitious, impossibly sexy man—she relished the idea of her parents giving him the third degree.

And they would. Both of them!

In the end, however, Natalie was forced to abandon that idea. It would be more trouble than it was worth. One look at Mike and her mother would start imagining that there was more to this marriage than met the eye. She knew her daughter's taste in men.

But she would still have to ring her mother tonight and tell her something to explain how she would soon have the means to pay off their mortgage.

A version of the truth came to her that just might work.

After she'd made herself a bite to eat Natalie made her way into the living room and reached for the phone.

# CHAPTER EIGHT

MIKE was sitting on his balcony with his feet up, sipping a glass of Glenfiddich and watching the night lights blink on all over the city, when his mobile phone rang. Putting his scotch down on the side table next to him, he lifted his right hip up and slid the phone out of his back pocket, flipping the phone open on its way to his ear.

'Mike Stone,' he said, wondering who it could be. One of his contract programmers perhaps? No, not on a Friday night. It was probably Richard, warning him again to keep his hands off his prospective bride.

'Mike. It's Natalie.'

'Natalie!' His eyebrows arched in surprise. 'I was just thinking about you.'

'I'm sure you were,' came the caustic retort. 'Where are you?' she demanded to know with a degree of puzzlement in her voice. 'Wherever it is, it's rather quiet.'

'I'm at home.'

'Oh. I needn't have rung your mobile, then. Not that it matters. Well, I did what you wanted me to do. I told my parents the truth. You'll be pleased to know that we're expected at their place tomorrow for a barbecue lunch.'

'What?' Mike's knee-jerk reaction had his feet falling off the chair onto the floor with a thud.

'I could have warned you this might happen,' she went on blithely. 'My parents happen to care about me. Naturally, they want to look you over, make sure you're not a psychopath, or a pervert. Which you might well be, come to think of it. I don't know all that much about you.'

'I am a lot of things, but a pervert is not one of them. I'm not a bloody psychopath, either.'

'How do I know? I only have your word for that.'

Mike bristled. 'I'm no saint, but I never lie. Ask around. You'll find that Mike Stone is a man of his word.'

'And who should I ask? Besides Richard Crawford, whom you admit has shares in your company and will benefit if I marry you and you get that partnership. That could be called a conflict of interest.'

'*If* you marry me? I thought it was a done deal.'

'That was before you brought my parents into it. Now, you'll have to pass muster with my mum and dad first. If you do, I'm all yours.'

The provocative words were out of Natalie's mouth before she could snatch them back. She should never have made this call. Never have decided to torment Mike with what would have happened if she *had* told her parents the truth.

Thankfully, he was on the end of a phone and not able to see the guilty heat spreading over her cheeks.

Because, of course, those provocative words echoed her secret desires. She'd *love* to be all his.

No, that wasn't quite right. She'd much prefer for him to be all hers. Her own private toy boy, to be played with till these cravings he evoked in her were satisfied.

But that was a pipedream. Total fantasy world stuff. The real world didn't allow women that kind of privilege. Women always paid for their sexual pleasure, with emotional involvement and the most soul-destroying pain.

It was only the men in this world who could take what they wanted, then walk away without turning a hair. Natalie didn't doubt that Brandon hadn't lost any sleep over her. He'd have just gone back to his wife, then eventually found another gullible female to sleep with on the side.

'The trouble with you,' Brandon had said to her scathingly when she'd told him to leave, 'is that you take life too seriously.'

Remembering those words reminded Natalie that she wasn't capable of playing sexual games. For her, lust and love inevitably became entwined. Whenever she went to bed with a man, she ended up falling in love with him. Brandon had not been her first disaster. Just her last.

*Definitely* her last, she reaffirmed.

'Before your testosterone gets any ideas,' she added in what she hoped was a suitably droll tone, 'that was just an expression.'

'I think my testosterone is quite safe around you, Natalie.'

Oh, that hurt. That really hurt.

'I'm very relieved to hear that, Mike. But perhaps you should be careful when choosing my new wardrobe. Men are renowned for being notoriously shallow when it comes to sex. In the olden days it only took a flash of an ankle and they were frothing at the mouth.'

He laughed. 'I'd need a lot more than a flash of your ankle, sweetheart. Not that I'm a frothing-at-the-mouth kind of guy. I've had women stand in front of me stark naked and it hasn't got me going.'

'Poor Mike. You have a problem in that area?'

He laughed again. 'I sure do at the moment. But I aim to fix it later tonight.'

Natalie thought as much. He was going out on the town to pick up some little dolly-bird.

'Hope you use protection.'

'Honey, I always use protection.'

'Do you realise that you've called me both sweetheart and honey in the last thirty seconds?' she threw at him. 'I thought we had an understanding about that.'

'That's the trouble with you, Natalie. You think too much. You'd be far better off putting on some glad rags, going out and getting yourself laid.'

'Like you, you mean?'

'I have no intention of going out anywhere tonight.'

'But I thought…'

'See what I mean? You think too much. Incorrectly as usual.'

'You are an extremely irritating man.'

'And you are an extremely irritating woman.'

Her sigh carried total exasperation. 'I have better things to do than try to mix words with you. Before this goes any further, I have a confession to make.'

'That sounds ominous.'

'The thing is, I didn't really tell my parents the truth. There is no barbecue lunch tomorrow at their place.'

'Sorry. I don't get it.'

'I wanted to show you how complicated things could become if we start telling all and sundry that we're getting married. I realise you want our wedding to look real. But I'd like to be able to get a quiet divorce later without having to explain anything to my family. Wouldn't you?'

'I don't have any family to explain my actions to,' he replied, making her wonder about him again.

'What, none at all?'

'None at all,' he ground out in a way that stopped her from asking any more questions on the subject.

'What about your friends?' she asked instead.

'I only have two close male friends. Rich already knows the situation and Reece soon will. I'll be asking him and Alanna to our wedding.'

'What on earth for?'

'The photos. And the kudos. Reece is a very high-profile businessman and Alanna is having a baby.

Helsinger will be impressed that I have friends with brains, and solid family values.'

'Maybe, but I'll be embarrassed.' As much as Natalie liked Reece and Alanna, they were former clients. She didn't like them knowing she was marrying Mike for money.

'You? Embarrassed?' he scoffed. 'Never! You're tough as teak.'

Natalie stiffened. If only Mike knew.

'Not nearly as tough as you,' she countered tartly.

'True,' he agreed. 'So what *did* you tell your folks?'

'As much of the truth as I could. I told them all about you and your potential partnership deal with Mr Helsinger and that you were willing to pay me a million-dollar bonus if I could find you a wife in a day. Which I happily told them I did. I just didn't tell them that it was me.'

'That was very clever of you.'

'Yep, that's me. Clever as well as tough. So you're right, Mike. Your testosterone is quite safe with yours truly. Clever and tough are not attributes in a woman which turn men on.'

Mike wished that were true. Unfortunately, his male hormones hadn't been this stimulated in a long time.

Of course, his recent celibacy had to be part of his problem. But it wasn't the only reason for his constant state of arousal. That sassy mouth of hers turned him on no end. Not to mention her deliciously repressed body.

Mike smiled a darkly rueful smile. She'd really had him going there for a while over that barbecue business. He'd actually started to worry over what he'd tell her folks about his background.

As much as Mike preferred the truth, he'd have been forced to lie. Because the truth would have seen any normal, loving parents advising their darling daughter to have absolutely nothing to do with him, no matter how much money was involved!

The truth might send Natalie running for cover as well. He'd have to be careful with her, and around her, in many ways. Perhaps he should restrict seeing her till their wedding, cut down the odds of anything happening that might spoil things.

Yep. That was what he would do.

'By the way, I can't make it to the bank on Monday morning,' he said straight away. 'I'll drop in later in the day and sign the pre-nup.'

'Fine,' she said in her usual snippy fashion.

'We'll make the following Saturday our clothes-shopping day. I have to find out from the Helsingers what you need first. But we might as well make a time now. How about nine?'

'You mean I won't be seeing you till then?' came her astonished reply. 'What happened to making this engagement look like a real one? Shouldn't we spend a bit more time together? Go out to dinner occasionally. *Visit* each other.'

Mike could not think of anything worse. He was sure to end up making a pass.

'I don't seriously think Helsinger is having our

every move watched,' he said firmly. 'A man of his ego will rely on his own personal judgement. It's what we do on the yacht which will count, not our behaviour beforehand. See you next Saturday, Natalie.' And he hung up.

Natalie stared into her dead phone. She wasn't going to see him for a whole week.

That was seven whole days.

And seven whole nights!

'Good,' she muttered, and slammed the phone down.

# CHAPTER NINE

NATALIE could not believe how slow time went that weekend, and then the following week. She tried to keep busy, organising ads in magazines for Wives Wanted, as well as doing some spring-cleaning around the house. She visited her parents more than usual, delighting in their happiness over having their financial problems solved, but at the same time resenting Mike and his damned money every single moment.

The man was a menace all right. Not only had he revved up her hormones something rotten, he'd made her see how empty her life was. And how lonely.

She no longer enjoyed reading as much, or watching television. Yet she'd once really looked forward to sitting down with her latest best-seller, and watching her favourite TV shows. Suddenly, such activities seemed nothing more than futile time-fillers. Going to the gym felt pointless as well. Why shape and tone a body that no man ever saw?

As for working with the clients of Wives Wanted…

Matching people up together had seriously lost its gloss. Natalie decided that, once she got that second million, she would do something else with her life.

Meanwhile, her mind returned to tomorrow morning, as it had many times that day.

Nine, he'd said he would pick her up. Less than fifteen hours to go. So why did it feel like an eternity away?

Natalie found herself wandering through the house in a highly restless state, not settling to anything, her thoughts as agitated as she was.

At six-thirty, she decided to stop pacing and go down to Bertollini's for some pasta. Cooking herself something did not appeal.

Stopping in front of the hall mirror on the way out, Natalie scowled at her hair, which was up in a rather severe French pleat. Okay, so it was glossy and healthy-looking from a treatment the hairdresser had put in this morning. But Mike was right. Her hairstyle was boring. And ageing.

He was right about something else, too. She hadn't let her hair down—not in the way he meant—in a long time.

She shook her head and walked on to the front door, before grinding to an unhappy halt. The thought that Mamma Bertollini might ask her questions about her missing boyfriend was unbearable. So was the prospect that she might not ask at all, just look at her with pity in her eyes.

Natalie groaned.

The temptation to call Mike was acute, but she resisted.

Tomorrow was only one sleep away now. She could last. She *had* to last.

So where else could she go? Who else could she call?

She still had friends from her old job, she supposed. But she'd said no to their invitations to go to drinks on a Friday night with them so often that they'd stopped calling. Kathy had been her only close friend at work, but she was married now and expecting a baby. Natalie didn't want to visit her and see how happy she was.

Maybe she should go down to the local video shop and get herself a couple of new releases, as well as half a dozen chocolate bars. Boost her spirits that way. She might pick up some wine as well, and get plastered.

Her own phone ringing interrupted her waffling and sent her heartbeat into the stratosphere.

It wouldn't be her mother. Her parents always went to the club on a Friday evening.

It had to be Mike.

As Natalie raced to answer it it came to her that maybe he was going to put off tomorrow. If he did, she'd just die!

'Natalie Fairlane,' she said in a much less crisp voice than the one she usually used for answering the phone.

'Natalie. It's Alanna. Alanna Diamond.'

'Alanna!' Natalie exclaimed whilst she struggled to contain her disappointment that it wasn't Mike. 'What a nice surprise. How are you?'

'Marvellous.'

'Your memory is obviously still fine.'

Alanna laughed. She had a very nice laugh. Very

feminine. There again, she was a very feminine woman.

Unlike me, Natalie thought wretchedly. No wonder Mike avoids me like poison. If I were a man, I would, too.

'You know, I don't think I ever thanked you properly for dropping in that day,' Alanna said.

'It was the least I could do.'

'Not everyone would have bothered. Anyway, Natalie, that's not why I'm ringing. The thing is, I had a call from Mike earlier today.'

'Oh?' Natalie said tentatively.

'He told me about your coming marriage.'

'Did he?' He'd warned her that he would, but she still wished he hadn't.

'He's asked Reece and myself to help Richard and Holly with the arrangements for the wedding.'

Natalie tried not to feel hurt. And totally left out. But, darn it all, marriage of convenience or not, she was still the bride, wasn't she?

'I hope he explained that our marriage is just a temporary business arrangement,' she said sharply. 'Not some silly love match.'

'Yes. He was very emphatic about that.'

'I can imagine,' Natalie said drily. 'Mike made it perfectly clear right from the start that he's allergic to love and marriage.'

'I can just hear him saying that. But is that the case with you too, Natalie? Are you allergic to love and marriage? I mean…why start up a matchmaking service if you don't believe in romance?'

'I do believe in romance,' she confessed, 'but the reality of life has dented my faith in the opposite sex somewhat.'

'Yes, I know what you mean,' Alanna agreed, perhaps thinking of her first, rather horrific marriage. 'So this marriage to Mike is strictly a matter of money for you as well, then. You don't secretly fancy him, do you?'

Alanna waited for Natalie to say *of course not* in her usual businesslike fashion. But when there was no immediate answer from down the line, Alanna realised that maybe—just maybe—there was more to this marriage than met the eye. At least on Natalie's side.

'Natalie?' Alanna probed gently.

The sigh she heard was rather telling. It looked as if Holly *had* been right, Richard's wife having immediately put a romantic spin on Mike's coming marriage to Natalie.

'No decent girl marries a man just for money,' Holly had pronounced when they'd discussed the situation over the phone. 'If this Natalie is as nice a person as you say, then she must be attracted to Mike.'

'You do fancy him, don't you?' Alanna persisted.

Natalie sighed again. 'I have no idea why. He'd have to be the most irritating man I've ever met.'

'He is a hunk, though.'

'True.'

'So would I be mistaken in saying that the no-sex

side to this marriage doesn't meet with your approval?'

Natalie didn't deny it. 'It's no use wishing for the moon, Alanna. Mike's not attracted to me at all.'

'How do you know that?'

'He said so.'

'Oh, dear. He can be so tactless at times.'

'Tactless. But truthful. So tell me, Alanna, just out of curiosity, what kind of female does Mike usually date?'

'Difficult to say. They come from all walks of life. But they're always good-looking, with good figures.'

'I see…'

'*You* have a good figure,' Alanna pointed out.

Natalie laughed. 'I don't think it's a question of my figure, but my whole package. Aside from my too cynical and assertive manner, he thinks my hair lacks pizzazz and my clothes are appalling. He says he's going to have to take me clothes shopping before the wedding because he doesn't trust my taste.'

'Actually, no, he's not,' Alanna said.

'Not what?'

'Not taking you clothes shopping. I am. That's the other reason I'm ringing. Mike doesn't have the time. He's working.'

'But he said he was between projects!'

'Not any more. He's found some bug in his new program and he has to fix it. Sorry.'

'He could have at least called and told me personally!' Natalie snapped.

'You're absolutely right. He should have. I suppose

you were looking forward to Mike taking you clothes shopping.'

That was such an understatement. Natalie suddenly felt like a balloon that had lost all its air.

'I wanted to show him he was wrong about my being such a dag,' she confessed wearily. 'My silly pride again.'

'I don't think pride is silly at all. You can still show him, starting with your wedding day. I'd bet you'd like Mike's mouth to fall open when he sees you in your wedding dress, wouldn't you?'

Natalie didn't know what to say to that. She'd spent every moment since meeting Mike fighting her desires and telling herself not to make a fool of herself over him. But where had that got her? She was downright miserable.

If there was even a slim chance she could make Mike want her—even for one night—she was going to take it.

'Yes,' she admitted with a sigh. 'But do you honestly think that's possible?'

'Sweetie, you could knock him for a six. No trouble. By the time I've finished with you, Mike won't be able to keep his hands off. Aside from anything else, I have it on good authority that, come the first week in December, your groom will have been celibate for quite a few weeks, a most unusual occurrence for Mike. His testosterone level is going to be sky-high.'

Natalie winced. Did she really want Mike taking

# OFFICIAL OPINION POLL

## ANSWER 3 QUESTIONS AND WE'LL SEND YOU
## 4 FREE BOOKS AND A FREE GIFT!

0074823 | FREE GIFT CLAIM # 3953

### YOUR OPINION COUNTS!

Please tick TRUE or FALSE below to express your opinion about the following statements:

**Q1** Do you believe in "true love"?

*"TRUE LOVE HAPPENS ONLY ONCE IN A LIFETIME."*
- ○ TRUE
- ○ FALSE

**Q2** Do you think marriage has any value in today's world?

*"YOU CAN BE TOTALLY COMMITTED TO SOMEONE WITHOUT BEING MARRIED."*
- ○ TRUE
- ○ FALSE

**Q3** What kind of books do you enjoy?

*"A GREAT NOVEL MUST HAVE A HAPPY ENDING."*
- ○ TRUE
- ○ FALSE

**YES**, I have scratched the area below.

Please send me the 4 **FREE BOOKS** and **FREE GIFT** for which I qualify. I understand I am under no obligation to purchase any books, as explained on the back of this card.

P5KI

Mrs/Miss/Ms/Mr _____ Initials _____

BLOCK CAPITALS PLEASE

Surname _____

Address _____

_____

_____

Postcode _____

## The Reader Service™ — Here's how it works:

Accepting the free books and gift places you under no obligation to buy anything. You may keep the books and gift and return the despatch note marked 'cancel'. If we do not hear from you, about a month later we'll send you 6 additional books and invoice you just £2.75* each. That's the complete price – there is no extra charge for postage and packing. You may cancel at any time, but if you choose to continue, every month we'll send you 6 more books, which you may either purchase or return to us - the choice is yours.

*Terms and prices subject to change without notice.

her to bed just because his frustration had reached breaking-point?

The answer was as scandalous as their marriage.

Yes.

'I'll take your silence to mean you like the idea of Mike being unbearably randy, come your wedding day. Okay, so tomorrow morning we're going to start on our makeover mission. There's no time to lose. I'll pick you up at eight-thirty. Sharp. Ooh, this is going to be such fun.'

Fun. Natalie considered the word. It had been a long time since she'd had fun. *And* since she'd surrendered totally to the female within herself.

Suddenly, she felt more alive than she had in four long years.

# CHAPTER TEN

MIKE glanced at his watch. Ten past three and still no sign of the bride.

'Holly, go and see what's keeping Natalie, will you?' he said impatiently.

'Okay,' Holly returned amicably. 'But she's only ten minutes late, Mike. Brides are often much later than that.'

'But she's not a *real* bride,' Mike muttered after Holly left.

'Legally she will be,' Richard said by his side. 'Till you divorce her.'

Mike shot his friend a savage glare. 'Don't remind me.'

'What's the problem, Mike?' Reece asked from where he was standing on the other side of Richard. 'You're beginning to sound like you're having cold feet, like a *real* groom.'

'He will be a real groom,' Richard piped up again.

'Not exactly,' Reece said drily. 'He won't have a real groom's rights tonight. Which might be a problem.'

'And what does that mean?' Mike growled.

'I gather you haven't seen Natalie lately.'

'Haven't seen her in over a month.' He'd rung her twice, suggesting that he drop by, using the excuse of supposedly checking on her new wardrobe. But she'd always had some reason why it hadn't been convenient for him to visit, impossible woman that she was!

'Well, I have,' Reece said ruefully. 'She stayed over at our place last night. And all I can say is... good luck.'

When the bedroom door opened, both Alanna's and Natalie's heads whipped round to see who it was.

'Don't worry,' Holly said as she waddled in, her floaty pink dress doing its best to conceal that she was very, very pregnant. 'It's only me.'

'Just as well,' Alanna said, thinking to herself that her own bump was quite small compared to Holly's. Still, Holly was seven and a half months compared to her six.

'Wow, Natalie,' Holly gushed, her hands clutched across her big belly. 'You look simply fabulous! Doesn't she, Alanna?'

Alanna stood back to inspect the bride, smiling her satisfaction of a job well done. The dress was a triumph, the woman in it even more so. Amazing what the right clothes, make-up and hairdo could do.

Of course, she'd been working with excellent basic equipment. Natalie had a great figure, much better than her own slender curves. Her face had always had the potential to be striking, too, with the right make-up.

Changing her hair, however, had been the *coup de grâce*. Alanna had found an old picture of Rita

Hayworth and taken it along to a top city hairdresser to reproduce. The end result was a very sexy style, which fell in bangs and waves from a side parting to Natalie's shoulders. Her naturally auburn colour had been deepened with some more red, making her pale skin glow by comparison.

'I couldn't agree more,' Alanna said. 'If Mike doesn't go for you in this outfit,' she whispered in the bride's ear as she adjusted the ivory chiffon scarf around her head, 'then I'll go jump off the penthouse balcony.'

'You and me both,' Natalie murmured back.

'I can't believe you didn't buy that dress in a bridal shop!' Holly exclaimed. 'It *looks* like a wedding dress. Yet it's so original. I love the idea of the scarf instead of a veil.'

'Yes, it's most unusual,' Alanna replied. 'Ready, Natalie?'

Natalie looked away from where she'd been staring at herself in the mirror.

'As ready as I'll ever be,' she returned, and picked up the small spray of orchids that she'd chosen as her bridal bouquet.

God, she was nervous. Yet excited at the same time.

She felt, not so much like a bride, but how she imagined an actor felt on opening night on Broadway. For what was this but a performance? She was going out there, not just to marry a man, but to seduce one.

She hadn't set eyes on Mike since that Friday over

a month ago. She'd made sure she hadn't, deflecting him on the two occasions when he'd wanted to check on the clothes she and Alanna had been buying, then, today, making sure that the men didn't come to Richard's penthouse for the ceremony till she was safely in the guest bedroom, getting ready.

She and Alanna had been like two conspirators, plotting and planning.

Alanna had been right, though. It *had* been fun. Natalie was over the moon with the clothes they'd bought, not just her wedding dress, but her entire wardrobe. There was one evening gown in particular that she couldn't wait to wear.

Mrs Helsinger had emailed Mike their social itinerary on the yacht, which included this really swish yacht-warming party on the second night of their stay on board. Mike had given this itinerary to Alanna, telling her to make sure his future 'wife' had everything she needed.

On his part, Mike had taken Reece shopping with him to make sure *he* wouldn't let down his side in the clothing department. According to Alanna, Mike now had a wardrobe second to none.

'What does Mike look like?' she asked Holly.

'Fabulous. Just as good as Richard and Reece. Truly, it's amazing what a tux can do for a guy. But he's not in the best of moods. Very antsy. Shall I tell him you're ready?'

Alanna and Natalie exchanged meaningful looks.

'I think another five minutes, don't you, Alanna?' Natalie said, her heart thundering in her chest.

Alanna grinned. 'Maybe even ten.'

'Not that long,' Holly wailed. 'Please. I don't think *I* can stand it.'

Natalie smiled at Holly, whom she now counted as one of her friends. What a lovely girl she was. But such a hopeless romantic. She really thought something might come of this marriage.

Natalie suspected Alanna was harbouring a few secret hopes in that department, too.

But Natalie knew better. Even if she succeeded in making Mike want her sexually, he was not going to fall in love with her. A brief affair whilst the marriage lasted was all she could hope for. Even that was not a foregone conclusion.

Mike might take one look at her today and be downright furious. He'd told her at their first meeting that he didn't want to marry some *femme fatale* type who thought she could get him to change his mind about divorcing her afterwards.

Natalie's excitement took a nosedive with this train of thought, along with her confidence.

'That's all right,' she said, a sudden burst of nerves making her voice tremble. 'I don't think I want to wait that long, either. Tell Mike I'll be out in a sec.'

Mike frowned at Holly when she returned. 'Well?'

'She's coming out in a sec,' he was told. 'You'd better get ready.'

The three men and the celebrant—a dignified gentleman in his fifties—took up their positions near the railing of the penthouse terrace, which was a truly glorious setting for a wedding, especially on a warm summer afternoon with the sun shining and only the lightest of breezes. The view of the harbour and the bridge behind them was truly magnificent.

There would be no excuse for the photographer not getting great snaps of the bride and groom. Wedding photos were essential, if Mike was to convince Helsinger that the marriage was genuine.

At the moment, it felt all too genuine for Mike.

He'd been insane, coming up with this idea.

He didn't want to get married. He didn't want a wife, even a temporary one. And he sure as hell didn't want that wife to be a woman he wanted to take to bed as badly as this one.

Mike sucked in sharply.

*Oh, my God!*

That *couldn't* be Natalie Fairlane walking towards him, not in that long, slinky, stunningly strapless dress.

She didn't look like any bride he'd ever seen, despite the ivory colour. She looked like a temple goddess with that sexy scarf wrapped around her pale throat, then swathed around her simply stunning red hair.

Mike's feelings for Natalie had been controllable when she'd been dressed like a legal-aid lawyer. Suddenly, nothing was controllable. Not his desire. Or his anger.

She'd done this on purpose. Transformed herself in secret to catch him unawares. Perhaps to make him look a fool. She was a witch, like all women.

But she'd made a big mistake, taking him on.

He never made a fool of himself over a woman.

If she thought she could turn him on, then spurn him, she was in for a big surprise. If anyone did the turning-on and the spurning here, it would be him.

Natalie's step faltered when Mike smiled at her. She much preferred his shock of a moment before. That had been most gratifying.

His smile, however, was unnerving. Because it was the wickedest, sexiest smile she'd ever encountered.

Not a large smile. Just a small lifting of the corner of his mouth, accompanied by a look that most women only dreamt about. His dark gaze smouldered as it travelled slowly down her body, then up again, bringing a dryness to Natalie's throat and a swirling lightness to her head.

She swallowed, then carefully continued her journey across the terrace to where the ceremony would take place, forcing herself to project a cool façade, even whilst waves of heat rippled through her tensely held body.

Thank the Lord the bodice of her gown was heavily lined and boned, otherwise her scorchingly erect nipples would have betrayed her.

The photographer, she noted, was busy taking pictures, both of herself and the three men waiting for her. Holly had been right about them. They all looked great. But Natalie's eyes were only for Mike, who looked simply incredible. Still not handsome in the traditional sense, but sophisticated and suave and, yes, too sexy for words.

Natalie swallowed again.

'I see you've been hiding your light under a bushel,' Mike murmured as he held out his hand to her, his eyes locking with hers.

'I did tell you that I could look prettier,' she returned, struggling to keep her cool as she placed her hand in his.

How big it was, his fingers dwarfing her own, his palm feeling large and hard against her own soft, slightly clammy skin.

'Honey, pretty is not the word for you today,' he said with another of those sexy smiles. 'As you very well know...'

She might have rebuked him for calling her honey if she'd been capable of speaking. Instead, she just stared up at Mike, her heart pounding behind her ribs as she realised that she'd achieved her objective.

He wanted her. Really wanted her. She could see it in his eyes.

His fingers tightened around hers as he drew her round to face the celebrant, giving her another glimpse of his strength.

His physical power both frightened and excited her. He would be a dominant lover. Powerful and passionate and primal, taking no nonsense from her. She could see him now, stripping her quite roughly before throwing her onto the bed.

Such thinking robbed her of her breath, and her brains.

The celebrant launching straight into the ceremony was a relief, giving Natalie time to scoop in several deep breaths. But her thoughts remained totally scattered during the next ten minutes. She must have made all the right verbal responses. But she had no memory of their marriage at all. Not till that moment when the celebrant told Mike that he could kiss the bride.

That woke her up.

Mike was holding both her hands by this stage, the spray of orchids having long been handed to Alanna. He turned her to face him, staring deep into her eyes as he slowly, very slowly, lifted her hands to his mouth, pressing his lips, first to her grandmother's wedding ring, and then against each startled fingertip.

Shivers ran down her spine with every touch, her eyes widening with surprise.

This was not the kind of lover she'd imagined earlier. This was a man with finesse. And lots of erotic experience. As much as Natalie had thrilled to the fantasy of Mike acting like a caveman with her, what he was doing at that moment was also very effective indeed.

Already, she craved for him to take one of her fingers into his mouth, to suck on it. Her mind whirled with the mental picture of his sucking on other, far more intimate parts of her body, her lips falling open to provide more air for her suddenly panting lungs.

His eyes narrowed on her mouth, oh, so knowingly, his hands dropping hers to cradle her face. He was going to kiss her now. Properly.

Her lips stiffened at first contact with his—perhaps out of some lingering, long-held fear—but all too soon they softened and trembled apart, inviting him in. When his tongue slid down deep into the warm, wet orifice behind her teeth, her arms slid around his back, wanting him close, then closer still.

Natalie totally forgot where she was. This was what she'd thought about and dreamt about for the last month. Being in Mike's arms. Being able to kiss him and touch him.

His body felt as good as it looked. And he kissed even better than she could have possibly imagined.

Mike's abruptly putting her aside only a few seconds later came as a shock. So was the cold glare he gave her before turning away to accept everyone's congratulations, leaving Natalie to struggle helplessly with the aftermath of his kiss. Her heart was racing, her face felt hot, and her nipples were like bullets inside her dress.

She didn't know where to look or what to do.

Alanna and Holly producing some nibbles, plus trays laden with champagne-filled glasses, was a godsend, Natalie scooping up a glass brimming with the sparking liquid. She desperately needed something to help her regather her composure and face the depressing reality that she'd got carried away with herself earlier on.

Sure, Mike might think she looked sexy today. And, yes, he'd been very convincing in the role of besotted bridegroom in front of the celebrant and the photographer.

But it was now obvious that that was all it had been. A role. An act. He couldn't wait to stop kissing her. Or to leave her to her girlfriends and talk to his mates. Alanna had been wrong and she'd been right. She wasn't Mike's type. Never would be, no matter how much she tarted herself up.

'A toast to the bride and groom,' Richard proposed.

Natalie groaned a silent groan. So did Mike, by the look on his face. If only the celebrant and photographer would leave, she thought wretchedly, they could stop all this awful pretending.

More photos followed, and more toasts, Natalie's only relief coming from being able to replace her now-empty glass with another full one. She was infinitely grateful that she'd refused point-blank to have a wedding cake. Cutting it with Mike's hands clasped around hers in mock love would have been intolerable!

'I hate to hurry you,' the celebrant said at long last. 'But I have another wedding later this afternoon and have to drive some considerable distance to get there. So if we could please just sign the papers, I can be on my way.'

After he left, the photographer was despatched also, leaving the six friends alone. The atmosphere, however, was still not very relaxed. Mike had a face like thunder and Natalie just wanted to crawl into a bed somewhere and cry.

'I don't want to be rude,' Mike suddenly threw at his friends, 'but you've done your bit. The wedding's over. So could you please just go home?'

Natalie's mouth dropped open when his friends immediately did just that. Left.

Alanna and Holly did manage a brief parting hug, with Alanna whispering a hurried, 'Ring me in the morning,' but in no time flat she was alone with Mike.

'You might not *want* to be rude,' she snapped after he flicked the lock on the front door, 'but you *are* rude. A word of thanks might have been in order at least. Not a summary dismissal.'

His expression was equally dismissive of her. 'For pity's sake, don't be such a drama queen. My friends know the kind of man I am. *And* what I think of having to get married like this. The last thing they want is to be around me when I'm in a filthy mood.'

'I don't think much of it, either.'

'Too bad. You're stuck with me. Just think of the money, honey. You're getting well paid to put up with my moods for a while.' He snatched up an untouched glass of champagne and swigged back a hefty amount before glowering over at her. 'I do realise you thought today would end differently to this. But you thought wrong.'

Natalie stiffened. 'What do you mean—end differently?'

He walked slowly towards her across the thick blue rug that separated them, his eyes doing what they had done earlier, only much less respectfully.

'You thought you could play games with me,' he ground out. 'Teach me a lesson that my testosterone wouldn't forget.'

'I don't know what you mean,' she lied breathlessly.

He stopped right in front of her, his eyes now glittering and cold as he glowered down at her. 'You know exactly what I mean,' he ground out. 'You're a smart girl, Natalie. Smart and devious.'

'I wasn't playing a game,' she defended, the champagne having given her some Dutch courage. 'I just wanted you to see that I could look attractive, and sexy. Call it female vanity, but I didn't like you criticising the way I looked.'

'Let's call a spade a spade, Natalie. You wanted to turn me on. That's the bottom line.'

'All right,' she blurted out. 'Yes! I wanted to turn you on!'

'Well, you succeeded.'

Her whole insides contracted at his gruff admission.

'Not that it's going to do you any bloody good,' he added angrily.

Natalie was to wonder, afterwards, if it was the champagne that opened her mouth so boldly.

'I'm not after your heart, if that's what you're thinking. I just want your body!'

His lips pulled back into a cynical sneer. 'That's what lots of women say. But it's not what they mean.'

'Well, *I* do,' she insisted. 'Remember what you said to me the first day we met? You said that I needed you to sex me up a bit. You were so right. After the fiasco with Brandon, I'd fallen into shocking habits, with my dress and my attitude towards men.

But my worst habit was not staying sexually active. I was in danger of becoming a dried-up old maid. But when you came into my life, my female hormones got a wake-up call. You're a very sexy man, Mike.

'Not a man I could ever fall in love with, mind,' she hurriedly pointed out. 'Or want to stay married to. But a man I would like to go to bed with. Trust me when I say I *will* divorce you, once you've got your precious partnership.'

## CHAPTER ELEVEN

MIKE could not have been more taken aback. Damn it all, that was *his* speech. *He* was the one who usually said he wouldn't be falling in love, etc. etc. etc.

He should have been pleased, he supposed. The temple goddess had just given him the green light to sleep with her, without any strings attached.

So why wasn't he jumping at the chance? Why wasn't he already ripping that infuriating dress right off her and getting down to business?

Darned if he knew what was going on in his head. Or was it hers he was still worried about? Women could never be totally trusted. Mike didn't like it that Natalie had already got under his skin. He sure as hell didn't like it that he was going to ignore his misgivings and do what she wanted.

Resisting her, now that she'd offered herself to him, no strings attached, was impossible. He looked at her mouth and couldn't wait to make it melt under his—as it had when he'd kissed her earlier. He couldn't wait to hear her moan.

He'd liked the way she'd clung to him earlier as well. Liked it when her fingertips had dug into his back.

You like her too much, came the warning.

Too late!

'Fine by me,' he muttered, and reached out to start unwinding that tantalising scarf from her head.

By the time he tossed it aside, she was breathing heavily, her chest rising and falling. His own heart was going like the clappers. As he twisted her round to attack the zip at the back of the dress he told himself to calm down, to take his time. After all, she was his, not just for tonight, or a mere week, but till he divorced her. His to play with and to possess. Over and over and over. He could make all those fantasies he'd been having about her come true. Every single one.

By then, he should have had enough of her. *More* than enough, he reassured himself.

Mike breathed in deeply and glanced around, his hands stilling on Natalie's silky shoulders. Richard's penthouse was a fabulous place. Big, bright and airy, with a relaxed décor and a holiday atmosphere.

But the living room wasn't the ideal place for the kind of sex Mike had in mind. The tiled floor was cold-looking, and the cane furniture wasn't big enough for two people in the throes of passion, especially one his size.

His eyes dropped briefly to the blue rug underfoot, which was quite large and thick. The thought of pulling her down onto the floor had his flesh twitching. But he resisted the urge to indulge in something that could be counter-productive. Lots of women didn't go for that sort of thing. No, he needed a bed. King-sized.

There was everything he needed in the master bedroom. He'd been in there earlier, dropping off his overnight bag. The bed was huge, and the *en suite* bathroom spacious, with a corner spa bath and a shower built for two. Ideal settings for the sexy scenarios that had been tormenting Mike ever since he'd met Natalie Fairlane.

Mrs Stone now, he reminded himself. Mrs Mike Stone.

She was his, legally.

*His.*

A shudder ran through Mike at this thought, his hands tightening possessively over her bare shoulders. His mouth descended to push aside her hair and brush against the soft skin at the base of her throat, his nostrils flaring at the musky perfume she was wearing. When her head tipped back against his shoulder with a soft moan, he almost lost it, and, yes, almost dragged her down onto the rug with him.

But he steeled himself against temptation just in time, whirled her round and scooped her up into his arms.

Natalie gasped.

'Where are you taking me?' she asked breathlessly as he began to carry her in the direction of the bedrooms with considerable speed.

His smile was the smile of the devil. 'Somewhere a little more comfortable.'

'Oh…'

'Unless, of course, you like your sex on the rough side. *Do* you?' he demanded to know, grinding to a halt in the middle of the hallway. 'Be honest with me. Best I know right from the start what you like and what you don't like.'

She stared up at him, her mind flooding with lots of different scenarios, some rough, some tender, some slightly kinky. *All* of them exciting.

'I think I'm going to like everything,' she confessed, shocking herself, *and* him.

But Mike's shock only lasted a second or two before he laughed, a deep, throaty, sexy laugh. 'You're my kind of girl, then,' he said, and strode on down the corridor, steering her through the last doorway into what had to be the master bedroom.

When Natalie had first arrived at Richard and Holly's penthouse earlier in the day, she hadn't been interested in any grand tour. Her entire focus had been on getting herself ready and in steadying her nerves. So she hadn't been in here before.

Her eyes darted round the room, which was spacious and summery-looking, with the same cream tiles on the floor that ran through the whole penthouse, and the same cream walls. The furniture once again was cane, but painted white, not left natural. The bed was huge, with a blue satin quilt the colour of the sky. The wall that faced the terrace was totally glass, no doubt with built-in doors that slid back. Gossamer-thin curtains rested at each end, fully drawn back, the abundance of light reminding Natalie that the sun had not yet set.

Nor would it for several hours, Natalie thought with a swallow.

She was about to be made love to in broad daylight, by a man who was her legal husband, but whom she didn't really know.

Was that what made the prospect so exciting? Was it simply a version of the *sleeping with a stranger* fantasy? Or was it something else, a place where Natalie didn't really want to go for a second time in her life?

Concentrate on the sex, she told herself as Mike lowered her feet to the fluffy white rug that stretched along beside the bed. Don't think about the man, or the future. Think about the here and now. Focus on the pleasure of his touch. The feel of his male body. And what it can do for you.

A lot, she thought with a shiver when his hands ran lightly up and down her arms.

'You can't be cold.'

'No,' she admitted tautly. 'Please don't talk, Mike.'

His eyebrows lifted. 'You don't like to talk during sex?'

'No.'

'Mmm. You really *are* my type of girl.'

Secretly, Natalie suspected she wasn't, but she was going to try to be. For what was the point of being anything else? She might have made Mike want her in a physical sense today, but he didn't want her in any other way.

'Got any objections to my undressing you?' he asked abruptly.

*Did* she?

What would his type of girl do?

She recalled Alanna having told her that one of Mike's girlfriends had been an exotic dancer. Certainly no shy violet when it came to exposing her body. Natalie's stomach contracted as she whirled to boldly present her back to him.

I can do this, she told herself. I was once the mistress of a spy!

But the moment he started running the zip down her back and the tightly boned bodice was released, her hands grabbed at the gaping top, pressing it back against her swollen breasts.

But he would have none of her modesty, removing her hands quite forcibly and pushing her dress down till it pooled at her feet, leaving her standing there in nothing but a lacy white G-string and open-toed ivory high heels.

Natalie didn't know if she felt excited, or embarrassed. Whatever, her face was flaming.

'That's better,' he muttered, his hands zeroing in on her breasts, his outstretched palms rotating over her nipples.

'Oh,' Natalie gasped.

She could not remember her nipples ever feeling so big, or so tight. They kept lengthening and stiffening, two exquisite peaks of sensations that began screaming for more.

He gave them more, taking them quite firmly between his thumbs and forefingers, twisting then tugging till they were burning. Till *she* was burning.

When he abandoned her breasts to scoop her up

into his arms once more, Natalie was beyond worrying about anything.

The satin quilt was cool against her back. Cool and sensual. He arranged her in the middle of the bed with her head resting on a mound of pillows, stopping to plant a hungry kiss on her mouth before standing up and just staring down at her.

'You are one very beautiful woman, Mrs Stone,' he muttered, then began ripping off his own clothes.

She watched, fascinated, as he exposed his magnificent body to her eyes. It was everything that—and more than—she'd imagined. He had superbly developed muscles and a shape to emphasise them. Broad shoulders and chest, a six-pack stomach, slim hips and the legs of a gladiator.

But it was what rose up between those legs that drew her eyes the most, and held them.

'And you are one very beautiful man, Mr Stone,' she couldn't resist saying, her voice low and husky.

'I thought you said you didn't like to talk.'

'I've changed my mind.'

He shrugged his broad shoulders. 'Whatever turns you on.'

Just looking at him turned her on.

He stood there and stared down at her some more, then down at her lace panties, then further down to where she was still wearing her high heels.

'Those heels are lethal weapons,' he growled, sitting on the edge of the bed and reaching for her feet. 'They have to go.'

'The panties too,' he added after her shoes hit the floor.

Natalie held her breath as he hooked his fingers under the sides of her lacy G-string and levered them over her hips, peeling them swiftly down her legs, leaving her with nothing to hide her sex but a small vee of damp curls. She found herself pressing her thighs tightly together, embarrassed, suddenly, by her total nakedness.

Thank God he bent down and kissed her again, kissed her and kissed her till all her shyness melted away again, replaced by a fierce need to have him on that bed with her, on top of her, inside her, filling that part of her that needed to be filled, oh, so desperately.

'Mike,' she moaned against his mouth when he finally let her come up for air.

'Mmm?' His lips rubbed over hers, one of his hands around her neck, the other trailing down to tweak a still-tender nipple.

'Just do it.'

His head lifted, his eyes searching hers.

'You sure?'

'Yes,' she choked out.

'I won't be a sec.'

It took him more than a sec to retrieve a condom from his wallet. More like thirty seconds. But Natalie didn't mind. Despite the intensity of her need, she enjoyed lying there, watching him, admiring his male beauty, thrilling to the thought that, soon, he'd be really making love to her.

No, not *really* making love, she told herself with a small lurch to her heart. Having sex with her.

The brutal reminder dampened her excitement a little, till she accepted that honesty was better than deception, especially self-deception. This had nothing to do with love. It was all about sex.

But that didn't mean it wasn't special. Already she felt more of a woman than she had in years. A beautiful, desirable woman, a woman another man might want to get to know and love and possibly marry some time in the future. Being with Mike was going to be a changing experience in her life.

She was smiling up at him. Not a saucy smile. Or a sexy smile. A warm, soft, glowing smile.

Mike wasn't used to women smiling like that at him in bed. Not *before* he had sex with them. He wasn't sure what it meant.

He climbed onto the bed and kissed her again, obliterating the smile, bringing his mind and his body back to what he did understand. She wanted him to do it to her. Right now. No more foreplay. No fancy moves. Just straight into it.

Well, that was fine by him, he thought as his mouth turned savage on hers and his right knee wedged between hers, levering her thighs open. He could do that.

One hand twisted in her hair, holding her mouth captive under his whilst his other hand guided his straining erection into her.

Was it her moan he heard? Or his own?

Her flesh enclosed his like a soft leather glove. Restricting. Delicious. Exciting.

*Too* exciting.

Once buried in her to the hilt, Mike forced himself to lie still, lifting his mouth from hers and levering himself up onto his elbows.

She looked up at him dazedly, her beautiful blue eyes dilated with desire.

How seductive she looked, with her glorious red hair spread out around her flushed face; her lips wet and shining, and provocatively apart.

'Put your arms up above your head,' he told her.

She blinked once, then did it, the action raising her lush breasts, bringing her long, hard nipples closer to his mouth. But he didn't kiss them. Or lick them. Even though he knew she would have liked it. He didn't want to give her too much too soon. Or himself, either. He wanted to savour her. Like a wonderful meal. This was just the first course. The entrée. There would be many more courses to come. To hurry would have been a crime.

If only she hadn't moved her hips, and her bottom, her restless need compelling *him* to move, at first with creditable control, but then more urgently as hot blood rushed through his body, bringing him swiftly to that point of no return.

Soon, he was balancing on that knife edge, trying desperately to hang on, to satisfy her first. Her eyes were now tightly shut and her head had started twisting from side to side. Suddenly, her body lengthened under him, her arms stretching up till her fingers reached then slipped through the cane bedhead. She moaned, her back arching, her flesh squeezing tightly around his. The effect was electric and instantaneous. He could not possibly last much longer. Any second now he was going to explode.

She gave a tortured cry, then started spasming wildly around him.

Mike had never felt a woman come so intensely. His own answering orgasm stunned him as well, releasing his physical frustrations with a raw rush of pleasure that far exceeded anything he'd ever experienced before. Suddenly, he needed her closer, his arms sliding around her back to scoop her up from the bed. He sat back on his haunches and pulled her hard against him, her bottom balancing on his thighs. His mouth burrowed into her hair, pushing it aside so that he could suck on the base of her throat. She shuddered in his arms, her head tipping sideways to give him better access to the pulse in her neck, like a victim offering herself up to her vampire lover.

Eons later, they collapsed on the bed together, lying there for ages without saying a word, their ragged breathing taking a long time to calm.

'No, don't go,' she pleaded when he eventually went to withdraw.

Normally, once he'd had a woman, especially for the first time, Mike made a point of distancing himself, either by rolling over and going to sleep, or going to the bathroom.

Experience had taught him that danger lay during the blissful time of post-coital satisfaction. Women were extra vulnerable after sex and prone to misinterpreting his feelings for them. They invariably wanted to cuddle and to talk. Mike was not a talker, or a cuddler. The one time he'd been fool enough to do that—out of teenage gratitude—the girl had declared her love for him before he could say boo.

Mike couldn't stand being told by a woman that she loved him.

So why wasn't he bolting for the bathroom right now? Why was he stroking Natalie's hair gently back from her face and kissing her lightly on the lips?

Because this situation was different, he reassured himself. Natalie would never tell him she loved him. He didn't have to tread any careful line with her. He could relax and just do whatever he liked.

And he *liked* doing what he was doing at the moment.

'Want to come to the bathroom with me?' he suggested.

She looked slightly taken aback, as though no man had ever suggested such a thing to her.

'Er…what did you have in mind?'

'There's a great corner spa bath in there.' And he nodded towards the *en suite*.

'Well, I…'

'You get the champagne and nibbles,' Mike commanded. 'And I'll run the water.' He wasn't going to let her do what *he* usually did. Run for cover. 'We're married, remember? Having a bath with your husband is pretty normal behaviour for newly-weds.'

She laughed. 'Nothing about this marriage is normal, Mike.'

He shrugged. 'So? We might as well have some fun while it lasts. Isn't that what you want? To have fun? I'll let you wash me all over, if you'll let me return the favour.'

'You're wicked; do you know that?'

'Yep.'

She sighed voluptuously as she wriggled a little, making Mike aware that he was already on the road to recovery.

Hopefully, there'd be some more condoms in the bathroom. He only kept two in his wallet.

'Bingo!' Mike exclaimed five minutes later.

There was an open box in one of the vanity drawers, with several left inside. He began whistling as he turned on the bath taps and tipped in some bubble bath that was sitting on a shelf, then went in search of a few more fantasy-fulfilling items.

The very well-appointed bathroom supplied everything Mike had in mind.

All he needed now was Natalie.

'Natalie?' he called out. 'Where in hell are you?'

She came sailing through the open bathroom door, wearing an ivory silk robe, which she must have brought with her but that did little to hide her nakedness underneath.

'I can't open the champagne,' she said a bit breathlessly. 'I'm utterly hopeless at that kind of thing. Oh! Bubble bath! How lovely!'

She didn't look at him. Not directly. Mike didn't

think it was his nakedness bothering her so much as his erection.

Her sudden shyness was a bit of a worry. Maybe she wasn't as sexually experienced as he'd been imagining.

But that didn't make sense. Natalie had been a married man's mistress. They must have got up to some tricks together.

'Why don't you pop yourself into the bath?' he suggested smoothly. 'I'll get the champagne.'

'Oh, would you?' she said, looking at him at long last.

'Anything for you, beautiful,' he returned.

Her blush enchanted him. But he wasn't going to be totally fooled by it. She was one hot babe, once she got going. And he aimed to keep her going.

Reaching out, he undid the sash on her robe and slipped it back off her shoulders, letting it drop to the tiles. She sucked in sharply, but she didn't try to cover herself with her hands.

'I prefer you naked,' he pronounced, snaking an arm around her waist and pulling her against him.

She didn't say a word. Maybe she couldn't. Her eyes looked dazed. Mike felt somewhat rattled himself.

One feel of her lush body and his desire soared. He wanted her again. Now. Fast.

Thank the Lord the condoms were handy or he might not have bothered.

He didn't ask permission, her lack of protest confirming what he'd begun to suspect about her. She liked a man to be the boss in the bedroom. To take, not to talk.

He hoisted her up and onto the vanity in a flash, spreading her legs and pushing into her with one almighty thrust.

The silken glove of her flesh encapsulated him once more, holding him tight before drawing him in even deeper. He groaned to find that his orgasm was already building. He grabbed her hips, determined to slow things down a little. Instead, his rhythm was urgent, his eyes fixed on that spot where his flesh entered hers.

When she moaned, he glanced up at her face, then simply could not look away again. Her eyes were shut, but her mouth was open, her head tipped back so that her hair fell away from her back.

She looked utterly abandoned and totally beautiful.

He was still watching her when she came, her back arching away from him, her palms pressing flat on the marble vanity top as her naked cries of pleasure echoed off the tiled walls.

His own orgasm surprised him, being no less powerful, despite his distraction. He shuddered into her with force, his body not stilling for ages. Finally, he was done, his forehead dropping to her chest as a huge sigh rattled from his lungs.

And he was like that when her arms wrapped tenderly around his head, her lips brushing against the top of his head.

'That was incredible,' she whispered. '*You're* incredible.'

For a few moments, Mike wallowed in her warmth, and her flattery. He might have wallowed more if his wariness about women hadn't warned him not to get too carried away.

Her delicious body had already acted like a powerful aphrodisiac on him, making him lose control. He didn't want to start losing his head as well.

'Thanks for the compliment,' he said, lifting his head, then lifting her off the vanity.

Now it was time to slow things down before the next course. Time for that long, leisurely bath together, and the task of discovering exactly how far his sexy new bride would let him go.

# CHAPTER TWELVE

'NATALIE! At last!' Alanna exclaimed. 'I've been dying for you to ring me all morning. Still, I suppose it is only ten o'clock. Well? What happened after we left yesterday? Did he or didn't he?'

'Did he or didn't he what?' Natalie teased.

'For pity's sake, girl, don't torment me. I can already tell something happened. You sound too chipper for all our efforts to have failed. I want to know every single detail.'

Natalie laughed even as she blushed. No way would she be telling Alanna *every* single detail. *She* could live with the knowledge that Mike had rendered her absolutely shameless. But she didn't want anyone else to know.

Still, there was no point in pretending that she and Mike hadn't become lovers. He'd probably tell his friends. Men did like to brag about their sexual conquests.

And, brother, she was a sexual conquest to end all conquests! Was there anything she hadn't let him do last night? If there was, she didn't know about it. By the time he'd carried her out of that decadent bath, she'd been totally corrupted.

'Okay, okay,' she admitted. 'Yes, all our efforts worked. Mike and I did go to bed together last night.'

My, what a delicate way of putting it, considering their sexual escapades hadn't been exactly confined to the bed.

'I knew it!' Alanna exclaimed. 'Reece said he wouldn't be able to resist you. He said Mike and celibacy just don't go together.'

Natalie winced. As much as she knew she would never have been Mike's first choice of partner, she still didn't like to think it was just frustration that had compelled him to accept her offer of sex.

'So, what do you think of him now?' Alanna persisted. 'Do you like him any better?'

Natalie grimaced. She should have known Alanna would start asking questions like that. Natalie had suspected all along that both she and Holly had been harbouring hopes about this marriage.

But Natalie refused to encourage her friends. Or her own silly self.

'I guess so. But we have absolutely nothing in common.'

'Opposites attract, you know.'

'Attraction is not enough for marriage, Alanna.'

'It's a start. Do you think you might fall for him in time?'

'I don't think that's likely,' came Natalie's hedging answer.

Sexually obsessed with him, yes.

Addicted to his body, yes.

Falling in love with him?

Oh, dear, she sincerely hoped not. To self-destruct a second time over a man would be the final straw.

But Natalie suspected that, down deep in that place where unbearable truths tried to hide, she was already treading a fine line between being in lust and falling in love.

'Unlikely, but not impossible?' Alanna suggested.

'Nothing's impossible.'

'Where is he now?'

'He drove over to his place to collect the rest of his clothes for our stay on the yacht. And to buy some supplies.'

'Really? What kind of supplies? Holly said the penthouse had everything you might need for a short stay.'

Natalie could hardly say more condoms. That would be a dead give-away and lead to more awkward questions.

'Just the Sunday paper,' she replied. 'And some milk. We both like fresh milk in our coffee.'

'See?' Alanna said. 'You do have something in common.'

'You are an eternal optimist, Alanna.'

'Life without optimism is dreadful. You have to always have hope. I know what it's like to live without hope and it sucks. Holly and I were talking last night and we both think you're the right kind of woman for Mike.'

'Good heavens, why?'

'You're smart and sexy and extremely sensible. I'll bet you're a good cook, too.'

'I'm competent enough in the kitchen,' she admitted.

Brandon had been keen on cordon bleu food, but not so keen on paying for it. She'd spent hours making elaborate meals for him, often having to eat them alone when he hadn't turned up at the last minute.

'Just as I thought,' Alanna said. 'You're perfect wife material, Natalie. Now, all you have to do is make Mike appreciate that having a wife like you would be a bonus, not a burden.'

'What if I don't want Mike as my husband?' she retorted.

Alanna laughed. 'I've spent the last few weeks with you, Natalie. I think I know you quite well by now. Do you know how much you talked about Mike?'

Natalie groaned. 'How much?'

'Endlessly. Every time you tried on an item of clothes, it was…would Mike like me in this? Will this turn Mike on?'

'That's just sex, Alanna.' If she kept saying it, she just might believe it.

'Till it turns into something else. Mike's a good man, Natalie. And terribly lonely. He needs someone to love him.'

'He doesn't think so. He couldn't have been more adamant about not wanting love and marriage.'

'Try looking past that macho, loner act to the real man underneath. He's not as tough as he pretends. Do you know about all the money he spends on under-privileged boys? Boys who don't have much in the way of family, or money.'

'No,' Natalie said, startled by this piece of news. 'He's never mentioned that.'

'He wouldn't. But he gives heaps to these kids every year. Pays for them to go to summer camps. Buys computers for them by the bucketload. Goes to their schools and gives free computer classes. Recently, he started a new project, building community clubs for them. The kind that have indoor sporting facilities and games rooms and lots of other activities. Reece and Richard help out with donations, but Mike's money is the main source of finance. If you think he's going after this partnership deal to increase his own personal wealth, then you're dead wrong.'

Natalie was stunned. 'Why didn't you tell me this before?'

'I just didn't think of it. We were too busy trying to make you over into a sexpot. But now that you know, does Mike being a closet philanthropist make any difference to your feelings for him?'

'I…I…well, it sure makes me want to know more about him. I mean, what drives him, Alanna? What happened during his own childhood to make him the way he is? Do you know?'

'No. He never talks about it. Not even to Reece or Richard.'

'Must have been pretty bad.'

'*Very* bad, I'd say. Why don't you ask him one day, when he's…shall we say…vulnerable to a bit of pillow talk?'

'Mike's not into pillow talk.'

'Maybe you should ask him straight out?' Alanna suggested. 'After all, you will need to know something about his past before your stay on that yacht. Mr Helsinger or his wife might ask you about Mike's background, and it would look funny if you knew nothing.'

'Yes, I guess it would,' Natalie agreed, sounding calm whilst inside she was anything but.

Alanna was beginning to agitate her. And to make her think too deeply about Mike, plus her feelings for him.

Natalie refused to start acting as she had in the past, always thinking she was in love, always wanting more than the current man in her life was prepared to give. Common sense told her to settle for enjoying whatever time she had with Mike, especially this coming week.

Meanwhile, she didn't want to talk to Alanna any more. Or anyone else, for that matter.

Natalie felt infinitely relieved that she'd told her mother she was going away on a week's driving holiday down the coast and was turning her mobile off. She'd emailed the same thing to all her clients at Wives Wanted.

'I must go, Alanna,' she said. 'Mike'll be back any moment. Look, I won't ring again till next weekend. I'm not taking my mobile on the yacht with me and I'll be with Mike all the time. It could be awkward.'

'That's all right. You have a good time, now. Can I tell Holly about you and Mike?'

'Only if you don't romanticise the situation.'

'But it *is* romantic, Natalie. You just can't see it yet.'

'No, it's you who can't see it, Alanna. I'm *not* in love with Mike. It's just sex. Okay?'

'If you say so,' Alanna trilled whilst Natalie rolled her eyes. Some people just wouldn't listen.

'Goodbye, Alanna.'

'Bye, sweetie.'

Natalie hung up with an exasperated sigh. 'That girl,' she muttered.

'Alanna trying to do your trick, is she?'

Natalie whirled to find Mike standing in the doorway of the kitchen, his dark eyes watchful and wary.

'I didn't hear you come in,' she said before realising that she wouldn't have. The penthouse was huge and the kitchen quite a way from the front door.

On top of that, Mike's feet were bare.

A good lot of him was bare this morning, his only clothing a pair of bone cargo shorts, slung low on his hips.

'What do you mean?' she added with a frown. '*My* trick?'

'Matchmaking.'

Natalie pulled a face. But there was no point in denying what he'd obviously overheard. 'She only wants the best for you, Mike. She thinks you could do with a real wife. She also thinks I'm in love with you, just because I slept with you. I tried to tell her that she had it all wrong.'

'Yeah, I heard you say it was just sex.'

If that was the case, why didn't he look happier about it? Just sex was all he wanted from her, wasn't it?

'What is it with you women?' he ground out, marching over and plonking the milk and paper down onto the black granite counter top. 'Do you have to tell each other *everything*?'

Natalie's chin shot up. She would not be spoken to like that, certainly not by Mike.

'Pretty much,' she said. 'We women have this awful tendency to need people in our lives. For things other than sex, that is. We need companionship and caring and children and, whoops, oh yes, occasionally we need love. We are such silly fools! But don't you worry, Mike. I won't be looking for love with yours truly. I'm not that much of a fool. I can see you're frightened to death of the word. You couldn't love anyone if your life depended on it!'

He glared at her, his eyes glittering, his hands balling into fists at his side.

'You don't know what you're talking about.'

'Then tell me. I'd like to know. What drives you, Mike? Why are you generous with your money but not with your feelings? What happened to you when you were a boy to make you the way you are?'

He looked furious for a second, but then he laughed. 'I see Alanna has been telling secrets out of turn.'

'Being generous and kind shouldn't be kept a secret!'

'What I do with my money is my business and my business alone.'

'Which is what you're always going to be, Mike,' she snapped. *'Alone.'*

'That's my choice.'

'It surely is. I'm sorry, but I don't think I can continue with our sexual relationship.' Even as she said the words, she wished she hadn't.

His nostrils flared. 'Why not?'

'I…I'm not sure I can handle it.'

'You handled it well enough last night.'

'Don't be nasty.'

'I'm not being nasty. I'm telling the truth. Here,' he said, snatching up both her hands and spreading them over his bare chest. 'You couldn't get enough of this last night. Or of me. Nothing's changed this morning, Natalie. I'm still the same man and you're still the same woman.'

But I'm *not*, she wanted to scream at him. And you're not.

Something's changed between us, can't you see it? Can't you *feel* it?

'I certainly haven't had enough of you,' he growled.

Even as he said the words his eyes betrayed more needs than sexual ones.

Alanna had said how lonely he was, how he needed someone to love him. She was right. Natalie saw the truth in his face, glimpsing the emotional bleakness behind his physical passion.

But he would never admit it. She knew that, too. The wounds of his past—whatever they were—had never healed properly. All she could offer Mike was comfort in its most primitive form. She could not tell him she loved him, but she could show it.

'That's nice to hear,' she murmured, trailing her fingertips over his male nipples till they tightened into tiny marbles.

When her head bent to lick them he groaned, taking an unsteady step backwards till his back was pressed up against the kitchen benchtop.

'Is this what you want?' she whispered as she went down onto her knees before him, her eyes lifting up to his tortured face.

He sucked in sharply when she unsnapped the waistband of his shorts, moaning softly when her lips pressed against his navel. She swirled her tongue around it whilst her hands pushed his shorts and underwear to the floor.

How different it felt from when she'd done this last night. This was not an act of lust, but an act of love. Her hands cupped him gently whilst her lips ran lightly up and down his length. Every lick. Every kiss. Every touch. All done with love. And when she took him into her mouth, her head was swimming with emotion.

'No,' he ground out as he carried her from the kitchen in the direction of the bedroom. 'That is *not* what I want. I just want *you*, Natalie.'

Natalie didn't say a word as he swept her into the bedroom. She was too busy fighting with the futile hopes that his passionate words evoked in her.

Because he didn't *really* want her, did he? Not for ever. Just for the time being.

But the time being *was* exciting, she told herself as he lowered her to the bed.

*Enjoy it, Natalie.*

And who knew what might happen in the future?

Alanna had said that life without hope sucked.

Natalie had to agree with her.

So she began to hope.

# CHAPTER THIRTEEN

NATALIE was doing some last-minute primping and preening with her hair when she spotted Mike in the bathroom mirror. He was standing in the bathroom doorway, watching her.

Dear heaven, but he did look gorgeous in his new clothes. His cream trousers were superbly tailored, lending an elegance to his long, muscular legs. And she did so like the colour of his shirt. It was a deep fawn with a cream collar and arm bands that highlighted his tan. The shirt was short-sleeved, of course, showing off Mike's wonderful arms.

Reece had chosen well.

'Ready?' Mike asked her.

'As ready as I'll ever be,' Natalie replied as she whirled away from the vanity mirror. 'I didn't realise I'd be this nervous.'

'No need for you to be nervous. You look fabulous.'

'You like me in this?'

She'd wondered momentarily if Alanna had got it wrong, worried that she should have been wearing something more casual for her first meeting with the Helsingers. The white Capri pants she had in her case, for instance, not a calf-length skirt and matching top that were dressy enough for a day at the races.

'Blue suits you,' Mike said, pleasing her.

Wait till he saw the dress she'd bought for the party tomorrow night. It was bluer than blue.

'Pity about the bra,' he added as his gaze swept over her.

'But I'm not wearing a bra!' she said, confused by his comment.

'I know,' he said drily, his eyes zeroing in on where her naked nipples immediately peaked against the silk lining.

'Stop staring at me like that,' she told him agitatedly. This was what he was always doing to her. What he'd done continuously all yesterday. Turned her on with just a look. 'We…we have to be going in a minute.'

'No, we don't,' he growled. 'I can cancel and Helsinger can go fly a kite. There are plenty of other companies who'll want my program. I don't need Comproware.'

'But they won't give you a partnership,' she protested, thrown by this sudden change of attitude. 'Mike, you *married* me to get this deal. This is where the big money is, money you can do so much good with.'

His eyes narrowed on her. 'Are you sure you're thinking of my good works, or your own second million?'

Natalie stiffened. 'That's not fair.'

'No, you're right,' he said, actually looking a bit guilty. 'I apologise. I'm not myself today. It's just that I hate jumping through hoops for any man, and

Helsinger has been making me do that. He wanted me married so I got married. Something I said I'd never do. I was thinking this morning how much I like being my own boss. I hate the thought of kowtowing to Chuck Helsinger.'

'You'd never kowtow to any man, Mike,' she said, and meant it.

'But I already have,' he grumped. 'And probably all for nothing!'

'What do you mean?'

'If Helsinger *has* been having me investigated, then we're already busted. I mean…any PI worth his salt would have found out that my new bride runs an agency called Wives Wanted. What do you reckon Helsinger would make of that? Only a fool would think our marriage was the real McCoy.'

'In that case he *isn't* having you investigated,' Natalie reasoned aloud. 'Or he'd have cancelled the invitation to join him on his yacht and taken back the offer of a partnership. I'll bet my house on it.'

'I hope you're right, Natalie. But I have a negative feeling about this. Maybe Helsinger likes to play with people's lives. Maybe he's bored with being a billionaire.'

'Life is full of maybes, Mike. We've gone this far. We have to see it through.'

Mike stared at her. She was right, of course.

But he still didn't want to. Helsinger wasn't the only problem in his head today. *She* was. This beautiful and intriguing woman who'd got under his skin right from the start, and who was fast becoming an obsession. A dangerous obsession.

Dangerous to his peace of mind, not to mention the peace of his body. He was different with her from how he'd been with other women. The more he had Natalie, the more he wanted her. His desire had become a compulsion. He was beginning to *need* her, with the same desperation that a man dying in the desert needed water.

Mike had once vowed never to need a woman. Not like that. Never like that.

'Mike?' Natalie prompted, her lovely forehead wrinkled into a frown.

'You're right,' he said sharply. 'We have to see it through.' Even if it drives me insane. 'But I'm not going to put up with any bulldust.'

'At least we don't have to *pretend* to be lovers,' she said, and smiled a softly seductive smile.

The effect on him was stunning, as if he were suddenly wrapped in a warm blanket on a freezing cold night. Hot blood charged along his veins, stirring his flesh.

Thank God they had to get going right away, otherwise he might have pounced on her.

'No more titivating,' he ordered her abruptly. 'Let's get out of here.'

'I have to get my handbag first,' she said. 'And the wedding photos.'

'No. Not the photos.'

'But you paid extra for a brag book to be delivered this morning so that you could show the Helsingers!'

'I've decided I do not wish to show them to the Helsingers. They're not close friends. They wouldn't expect it.' In truth, he'd hated the way the photographer had captured the way he'd looked at Natalie before and during the ceremony. Like some infatuated, fatuous fool.

'I'll meet you at the front door,' he said brusquely as he walked off.

He'd already taken their cases downstairs to the concierge of the building, there at the ready for when the hire car arrived. It was due at ten-thirty, booked and paid for by their host to escort them to where his yacht was moored at a pier at Darling Harbour.

A glance at his watch showed it was ten twenty-nine.

'Mike, what will I say if the Helsingers ask me questions about your family background?' Natalie queried on the way to the lift.

'Just tell them the truth,' he told her bluntly.

'But I don't know anything about you.'

'Exactly,' he said, and hustled her into the lift. 'Tell them you don't know anything about me.'

'But I can't say that. They'd think I'm crazy to marry a man I don't know anything about.'

'Mmm. They could be right.' He hit the button and the lift doors closed. 'Say I had a horrible childhood, but I don't like to talk about it.'

He could feel her looking at him, but he refused to look back at her. Things happened when he looked at her. Bad enough that her perfume was enveloping him in that closed space.

'And *did* you? Have a horrible childhood?'

He dared to look at her now that he had a reason to be annoyed. 'You're an intelligent woman, Natalie. You already know I did. Let's leave it at that, shall we?'

Natalie shivered under his harsh voice and suddenly cold eyes, so different from the way he'd looked at her earlier.

Any lingering excitement she might have been feeling over spending two romantic days with Mike on board of a luxury yacht faded to nothing. If he didn't change his mood, this was going to be more than difficult. It was going to be miserable.

But the sight of a white stretch limousine waiting for them outside the apartment building lifted Natalie's spirits.

Impossible not to feel some excitement when confronted by such luxury, plus the added little thoughtful touches inside. Champagne. Caviare. And a welcome message on the built-in television that the driver set into motion as soon as they were under way.

Even Mike smiled when their larger-than-life host filled the screen, introducing himself and his very pretty blonde wife before congratulating them on their recent marriage and saying how much he and Rosalie were looking forward to meeting them both.

'So what do you think?' Natalie whispered once it was over and the television went blank.

Mike pressed the button that operated the privacy screen, waiting till it slid into place before answering.

'I think any man who wears a navy blazer with brass buttons has *not* been having me investigated.'

Natalie laughed. 'He did look like an escapee from the fifties, didn't he? But I rather liked him.' Okay, so he was fat *and* bald. But he had a nice face. And happy eyes.

'What did you think of his wife?' Mike asked.

'Hard to form an opinion. She didn't say a single word.'

'I would imagine that making conversation is not Mrs Helsinger's role in Mr Helsinger's life,' Mike said drily.

'They might be very much in love,' Natalie suggested.

Mike's face showed a wealth of scepticism. 'You saw the size of him. She married him for his money and he married her for what she does when she's not talking.'

Natalie recoiled as her mind shot back to what she'd done for Mike a few times when she hadn't been talking.

'What is it?' he said sharply. 'What did I say?'

'Nothing. I…nothing.'

'No, it's not nothing. You look upset.'

Her eyes searched his. 'I…I just didn't want you to think that anything I've done with you has anything to do with money. Because it hasn't. I…I like you, Mike. I like being with you. Honestly.'

Natalie didn't know how else to put it without saying that she loved him.

He turned his head away to stare through the tinted window next to him. 'It *has* been fun, hasn't it?'

Natalie swallowed. He was talking in the past. Was that it, then? Had the boredom begun to set in? He certainly hadn't been bored with her earlier this morning.

Still, she'd sensed a change in him later. A cooling. And a distancing. He hadn't held onto her hand in the lift. Or touched her in any way for a while. Yesterday, he hadn't been able to stop touching her.

'Are you trying to tell me something here, Mike?' she asked him, determined not to cry. Or make a scene. If it was over for him, then it was over.

His head turned slowly back to face her. 'Like what?'

'Like we might have to *pretend* to be lovers from now on?'

'I don't think I could manage that,' he muttered.

'Manage what?'

'To be with you in such close quarters and not have sex with you.'

'Gee. I'm that irresistible, am I?' she threw at him.

He looked hard at her, his dark eyes glittering. 'Actually, yes, Natalie. You are.'

She sucked in sharply, her mind spinning at his admission.

'Nevertheless, come Thursday, I'm calling it quits,' he added, suspending her breathing altogether.

'But why?' she choked out.

'Because.'

'Because *why*?' she demanded to know.

'I have to stop this before you get hurt,' he ground out. 'I'm no good for you, Natalie. I'm nothing but a twisted, heartless bastard. I'm not interested in love. I'm not interested in anything but having sex with you.'

'So? You haven't heard me objecting, have you?'

He glared at her before suddenly reaching out to grab her upper arms and yank her hard against him.

'God damn you, Natalie,' he growled, his eyes cold and hot at the same time. 'God damn you to hell.'

But it was Mike who took her to hell, right there, in the back of that limousine. He didn't even undress himself. *Or* her. But she still came, with the same savage swiftness that he did.

Afterwards, he slumped back against the leather seat, total torment in his eyes.

'Why don't you ever say no?' he raged as he fixed his clothes. 'Why don't you ever stop me? You should have stopped me this time, Natalie. I didn't even use a condom!'

She just stared at him, her mind racing to dates, her heart jolting once she realised the possible consequences of his uncontrollable passion. No, not possible, *probable*. She was right in the middle of her cycle.

Surprisingly, no panic followed this discovery. Instead, a strange calm stole over her. A sense of karma.

'It's all right, Mike,' she told him as she opened her handbag and set about repairing any damage to her appearance. 'It won't be a problem.'

'You're sure?'

'Absolutely. I ovulated a while back,' she said. A minute ago, hopefully. 'You don't have to worry. Truly.'

And that *was* the truth. She would not burden him with a child he didn't want. If she was lucky enough to become pregnant, she would have his baby all by herself and love it to pieces for the rest of her life, just as she loved him.

'Oh, do stop scowling at me, Mike,' she added, her new resolves having brought a boldness with them. 'I'm not trying to trap you into anything. Okay, so I admit I'd like our relationship to continue for a while longer. You really are *very* good at sex. But I can see you're determined to end things when we leave the yacht. I won't argue with you. But there's no reason why we can't enjoy our time left, is there?'

He just shook his head at her, his expression approaching bewildered.

'I'll take that as a no,' she went blithely. 'Now, could you pour me a glass of that very expensive champagne? No point in wasting it.'

# CHAPTER FOURTEEN

THE Helsinger yacht was what was called an ocean-going super yacht. It was sixty-five metres long, with an aluminium hull, twin engines, computerised navigation systems and a top speed of seventeen knots. It accommodated twelve guests and fourteen crew. There were six deluxe guest cabins, a formal lounge and dining room as well as a large saloon and a home cinema with tiered seats and surround sound. The teak decks incorporated informal dining and entertaining areas along with a swimming pool, a spa, a games area, a heliport—complete with helicopter—and a twelve-metre launch, which doubled as a game-fishing boat.

Their host supplied all this mind-boggling information within minutes of Mike and Natalie boarding the *Rosalie*.

Chuck proved to be even larger in the flesh than he'd appeared on television. But he was holding his age well, as big men sometimes did. His wife didn't look a day over thirty. Clearly, she had an excellent plastic surgeon.

Mike actually didn't mind when Chuck swept him off for a hands-on, man-to-man tour of his pride and joy, leaving Natalie to be shown to their cabin by Mrs Helsinger, who'd swiftly proved she could talk.

Frankly, some time away from Natalie was just what the doctor ordered. Mike still hadn't totally recovered his equilibrium from the interlude in the limousine. He had never, ever been that carried away before that he hadn't used a condom. Aside from that, Natalie's ready agreement to their separating on Thursday did not sit well on him. Which was perverse. Neither did the way she was suddenly acting. As if she was on some kind of high.

Admittedly, she'd downed a tall glass of champagne before they'd pulled up on the pier at Darling Harbour. But that shouldn't have set her cheeks aglow the way they were glowing.

She'd never looked more beautiful, or more desirable.

Yes, best he keep away from her every chance he got during the next two days. Or at least make sure one of the Helsingers was around when they were together. There'd be no afternoon naps down in their cabin. Or watching movies alone in that incredible home theatre. Mike vowed to stay on deck as much as possible, in full view of the crew.

'You have to have a look at the bridge,' Chuck insisted after showing Mike the pool with its swim-up bar and huge spa.

The bridge was amazing, resembling something you might imagine gracing a spaceship. Mike was soon blessedly distracted with boy stuff, chatting away to the captain who pointed out all the electronic gadgets and gismos.

'So what do you reckon, Mike?' Chuck asked after

they left the bridge. 'It's a great boat, isn't it?' he added, waving his hands around the deck in an arc as expansive as his waistline.

'You're a lucky man.'

Chuck's laugh was as big as he was. 'You're the lucky man, from what I've seen. That wife of yours. Wow. She's a living doll.'

'Natalie's a wonderful girl.'

'How did you meet her?'

Mike looked into Chuck's far-too-sharp eyes before deciding he wasn't going to lie. As much as he did want the billions a partnership with Comproware might bring, he couldn't stand the deception. Or the pretence.

'Actually, Chuck, Natalie runs an introduction agency called Wives Wanted,' he said matter-of-factly. 'When I was told you wouldn't consider a business partnership with any man who wasn't married, I decided to find myself a wife, quick smart. So I gave Wives Wanted a call.'

Chuck looked totally taken aback. 'You mean you were prepared to get hitched, just to get a partnership with me?'

'It seemed a good idea at the time.'

'And?'

'Natalie refused to find me a wife on the basis of a business-only arrangement.'

Chuck was beginning to look a bit confused, which rather confirmed what Natalie had said. He hadn't had Mike investigated.

'I see,' his host said. 'Sort of. So what happened

next? Nope!' Chuck held up both his hands in a stopping gesture, his eyes twinkling. 'You don't have to tell me. I can guess. You took one look at each other and fell madly in love.'

Mike opened his mouth to deny it, then closed it again. It was perfectly clear Chuck didn't want to hear the truth. He wanted to hear romance. The man was an incurable romantic!

'How did you guess?' Mike said.

'Same thing happened to me. With Rosalie. One look and pow! She was driving this car—a snazzy little red convertible—and we pulled up next to each other at a set of lights. Her eyes slid over my way and that was it. Love at first sight. I had that girl in bed before the afternoon was out. Three days later, we surfaced and headed for Vegas.'

'Weren't you worried it might not last?'

'Nope. I knew it was the real deal, you see, the same way you knew. I'd already been married and divorced twice. To girls who had dollar signs in their eyes when they married me, not love. I knew straight away that what Rosalie and I had together was different. It wasn't just the sex. It was how I felt when I was with her. Like we were soul mates. I've never talked so much to a woman in all my life. Never felt so happy, either. Nope, neither of us had any doubts, despite our age difference. And here we are sixteen years later, as happy as pigs in mud, with two great kids and a lifestyle second to none.'

'Looks like you have it all,' Mike said.

'No need for you to envy me, my boy. You play your cards right and you'll have it all, too.'

'If playing my cards right means sucking up to you and your rather late-in-life moral standards, Chuck, then you've got the wrong man.'

Chuck threw back his head and laughed a big belly laugh. 'I'll have to tell Rosalie that. She'll crack up. She always said that one day I'd meet my match in the business arena. I think today might be that day. But don't worry, Mike. If anyone has to do any sucking up around here, it's going to be me. I'm told that this new firewall program of yours is going to revolutionise the worldwide web. Going to make someone a mighty big parcel of money, too. My lawyers are already working out a deal which will give both of us the best of that world.'

'I'll look forward to having *my* lawyers look at it,' Mike said, playing it cool.

But he couldn't wait to tell Natalie.

'I suppose you'd like to tell your little lady the good news,' Chuck said, making Mike wonder if he was a mind-reader.

'Yes, she'll be pleased.' *Very* pleased.

Now, she wouldn't have to wait long for her second million. Not the most inspiring thought.

Natalie would be the one who ended up having had it all. A satisfying sexual fling with him. And a nice pot of money to take with her afterwards, making her an even more desirable catch for some man who wanted what she wanted. Marriage and children.

Mike's jaw clenched down hard when he thought

of her marrying some other man. Of her smiling at him, and getting pregnant by him and being happy with him.

And where would he be whilst all this was happening? He'd be alone, as she'd said he'd end up being.

But wasn't he better off being alone? You didn't hurt anyone when you lived alone. You didn't destroy lives.

'I think it's time we joined the girls for lunch,' Chuck said. 'It's being served on the upper deck where we can get a good view of everything. The plan is to cruise around your magnificent harbour during lunch. After that, we'll be heading out through your heads and up the coastline to Pittwater. I'm told that's one of Sydney's most panoramic waterways. I dare say you've already seen it, being Sydney-siders, so while Rosalie and I act like typical tourists you two newly-weds might like to have a little lie-down.' And he winked at Mike.

When Chuck strode off in the direction of the steps that led down to the next deck, Mike shook his head. Everyone was conspiring against him. But what the hell? A little lie-down with Natalie might be a necessity by then, given he had to endure sitting next to her during what would probably be a long lunch, looking at the size of Chuck.

Launching himself after his fast-disappearing host, Mike decided not to fight the situation any longer. He was here with Natalie for the next two days. He might as well enjoy them, as she said.

*　　*　　*

'So what do you think of the Helsingers now?' Mike asked as he rolled over and picked up the remote control of the huge plasma-screen television that was built into the wall opposite their bed.

It was their first actual conversation since they'd retired to their cabin after lunch. Talking had not been an immediate priority on Mike's agenda, and, as usual, Natalie had been with him all the way.

When he rolled back, she snuggled up to him, running her fingers lightly through the smattering of curls that covered the centre of his chest.

'I really liked them,' she said. 'Impossible not to. Impossible not to like this boat as well. Just look at the size of this cabin. And the sheer luxury.'

Mike could not help but agree. The walls were wood-panelled in a rich, warm-coloured wood, the gold carpet on the floor thicker than any carpet he'd ever come across. The bed was simply huge, and, whilst its green and gilt brocade quilt was currently on the floor, Mike had to admit that it would not have looked stray in a palace. Neither would the *en suite* bathroom, which was made entirely in black marble with gold fittings.

The furniture all looked like genuine antiques, but possibly they were reproduction. Only the lighting was modern, being recessed to give the illusion of more space. The walk-in robe-cum-dressing-room was surprisingly large, and already hung with all their clothes by the time they'd come down, making Mike glad that he'd gone shopping with Reece.

'I like them too,' Mike admitted, flicking through

the satellite channels out of curiosity before turning the television off again. He had better things to do than watch TV.

'You were a big hit with Chuck,' he said, lying back and wallowing in the feel of Natalie's hands on him.

'That's nice,' she murmured.

'He virtually told me the partnership's mine.'

Natalie's head shot up. 'He *did*? Why didn't you tell me earlier?'

'Couldn't. My tongue was otherwise occupied.'

She laughed, then levered herself over to lie on top of him, resting her chin on her hands, which she'd folded over his heart. 'So it was. You know you're very good at that. Not all men are, you know?'

'Thank you for reminding me that I wasn't your first.'

'Don't tell me you're jealous.'

'Would that be a surprise?'

'Absolutely.'

'Then prepare to be very surprised. Because I'm very jealous,' he growled, rolling her over and pinning her underneath him. 'Of every man you've ever been with.'

'Don't make it sound like a legion. I haven't had all that many. Unlike you, Mike Stone.'

'Yeah, but I've never had a woman like you.'

'Is that a compliment?'

'It's a damned complication.'

'Why?'

'Because I don't want to let you go.'

There! He'd said it. Now let her make of it what she willed.

She stared up at him, her eyes stunned.

'Do you really mean that?'

'Unfortunately.'

'Why unfortunately?'

'Because I'm no good for you. You want a proper marriage. With children. I'm not cut out for anything proper. And I sure as hell don't ever want to be a father.'

'But *why*, Mike? You're wonderful to those boys you help. You obviously have a lot of love to give.'

'Love! I don't give them *love*. I give them help. And money. And opportunity. Love's got nothing to do with what I do.'

'Then what's it got to do with?' she threw up at him. 'That horrible childhood of yours, I suppose. You don't want other boys to go through what you went through, is that it?'

'Something like that.'

'So what *was* it that happened to you, Mike?'

'I told you. I don't like to talk about it.'

'Why not? It might do you some good.'

For the first time in his life, Mike was tempted. He sucked in a deep breath, but then shook his head. He just couldn't tell her. He didn't want to see pity in her eyes.

'What are you afraid of, Mike?' she persisted. 'I promise not to tell anyone else. This will just be between you and me.'

'Trust me. You don't want to know.'

He could just imagine how Natalie would react. She'd had such a normal childhood. She had no idea what it was like to live the way he'd lived as a kid. Okay, so her dad had obviously been a bit of a dill, money-wise. At least she'd *had* a dad. And a mother who'd been a mother. They actually sounded nice.

'Mike, I think it's important that you talk about what happened,' she went on, clearly determined to worm everything out of him. 'You've bottled it up for too long. If you're worried I might be shocked, then don't. I'm not some fragile flower. I've seen and read about lots of not-so-nice things in my life.'

He grimaced, then rolled over to lie next to her. Maybe he could do this if he didn't have to look into her eyes.

And maybe he couldn't.

'I wouldn't even know where to start,' he muttered.

'Let's start with your being born. Tell me about your mother and father. Who were they? How did they meet? Where are they now?'

He slanted her a wry glance. 'You're not going to shut up till I tell you everything, are you?'

'Nope.'

Mike would have been irritated to death if it had been any other woman badgering him like this. So why wasn't he with Natalie?

Because you *want* to tell her, that's why, supplied that inner voice that he'd been trying to ignore, but that would no longer stay silent. You want her to know what makes you tick. You want her to understand you.

'Don't say I didn't warn you,' he still felt compelled to say. 'Okay, so you want to know about my parents. Not much I can tell you about my father. I never knew him. Never knew his name, either. My birth certificate says father unknown. I gather he was an American marine, here in Sydney on R and R.'

'So your mother had an affair with a soldier and you were the result. That's not so terrible, Mike.'

'Look, let's not whitewash anything here. Mum was a junkie,' he told her harshly. 'Had been since she was fifteen. Her parents kicked her out of home around that time. Mum used to pick up all sorts of men when she needed money for drugs. Obviously, that night she was too high to think of using protection. That's how I came about.'

'Oh. I see.'

Mike read quite a bit in those softly delivered words. None of it good. He'd known she'd be disgusted.

'I told you it wasn't a pretty story,' he snapped.

'It's not an uncommon story, Mike. But it's still a sad one. Sad for you and sad for your mum. Poor thing.'

'Poor thing!' He sat up abruptly and glared down at this woman who dared to have sympathy for his mother.

'I was the one who was poor. Me and my poor little brother!'

'Brother!' Natalie sat up also, her hands lifting to push her hair back from her face. 'You said during your interview that you didn't have any brothers or sisters.'

'Tony was my half-brother. Lord knows who *his* father was. Mum admitted she didn't know. I reckon she only had us kids because we were good little money-spinners. Welfare pays single mums more for each child they have.' His face twisted as he battled the tortured feelings that always welled up when he thought of his mother. 'She was a hopeless mother. Nearly all of her money went on drugs. There was never much left for food, or clothes. Even worse, no money for medicine for Tony who was a sickly kid, right from the start.'

And there they were again, the memories of his boyhood, flooding back, bringing with them the dark demons that had haunted his dreams for years and that only went away when he was working, or having sex.

They'd been Mike's two escapes for years. Work and sex.

But there was no escape for him this time.

It had been a mistake to bare his soul. A *big* mistake.

Mike whirled round, swinging his feet over to the side of the bed, all the while battling the tumultuous feelings that were welling up inside him. Tears pricked at his eyes, but he refused to cry. Crying was for babies. And women.

'You have no idea what it was like,' he bit out. Had she ever gone to bed hungry at night? Or gone to school with no lunch, and wearing hand-me-downs that were too small? Or watched a little brother fade away before her eyes?

Her gentle hands on his shoulders almost unravelled him totally.

'No,' Natalie said softly. 'I don't. But I can imagine how unhappy you all must have been. You, your brother *and* your mother. Try to have some pity for her, Mike. Try to forgive.'

'I can never forgive her,' he grated out, his head shaking from side to side. 'She told us how much she loved us. All the damned time. She'd cuddle and kiss us, but she never looked after us. Her actions spoke a lot louder than her words.'

'She was sick,' Natalie insisted. 'And she had no support. Not everyone is as strong as you, Mike.'

'Don't make bloody excuses for her,' he snapped. 'She made her choices and Tony and I suffered for them.'

Natalie could understand his bitterness. Still, children did judge their parents harshly. She resolved not to be so critical of her own mum and dad in future. All in all, they'd been wonderful parents. Warm and loving and caring.

'So what happened to her?' she asked gently.

He laughed. A cold, empty sound. 'She died of an overdose, of course. I was nine at the time. Poor little Tony was just six.'

'What happened to you and your brother after that?' Natalie asked. 'Did your mum's parents take you in?'

'You have to be kidding. The authorities contacted

them, but they said their drug-addict daughter and her filthy offspring were dead to them. So we were fostered out. To different homes. I didn't get along with any of my foster families. So I ended up in a state institution.'

'An orphanage, do you mean?'

'Yeah. An orphanage.'

'Oh, Mike…'

God, he couldn't take any more of her pity. His head lifted, his back and shoulders straightening.

'It wasn't too bad,' he lied. 'There was this nice old guy there. A janitor. He was into computers in a big way and could see how much I liked them. Anyway, he gave me an old one of his one year for Christmas. Fred, his name was. Uncle Fred. I've never forgotten him.'

That part was true. He'd gone back years later to repay the man's kindness, only to find out that Fred had died a few months before.

'So that's how you got started in computers.'

'Yeah. I took to programming like a duck to water and never looked back. I never did get my higher school certificate. I refused to sit for exams. I was a rebellious beggar back then. But it didn't matter in the long run. I made it by myself.'

'That you did,' she said in a way that made him feel quite proud. 'But what happened to your brother, Mike?'

Mike grimaced. Women! They had to know the ins and outs of everything, didn't they? They couldn't let sleeping dogs lie.

'He died. When he was eight. Meningitis. His foster parents didn't recognise the symptoms till it was too late. They thought he had the flu. Poor kid never stood a chance.'

'That's terribly sad, Mike. I'm so sorry.'

'Now you know why I don't want to be responsible for a child's life. I couldn't bear it if I was a bad father.'

'But you wouldn't be. You'd be an exceptional father, for that very reason. You'd care more than most men.'

'Would I?' He could just as easily be a chip off the old block.

'Yes, you would,' she insisted.

Her arms wrapping tightly around him brought the most incredibly moving emotion. If only her seeming belief in him were real. If only he could trust it, and himself.

'Would *you* have a baby with a man like me, Natalie?' he heard himself asking her, his voice still holding scepticism. 'Would you, *really*?'

Her lips, which had been planting tantalising kisses over his back, stilled.

Mike could just imagine what was going through her head.

'I might,' she said at last.

Yeah…*right*.

He twisted round to look into her eyes. 'You're just saying that.'

'No,' she denied. 'I'm not. Do you *want* me to have your baby, Mike?'

His stomach swirled with a sudden nausea. 'Good God, no,' he denied gruffly. 'What I want is for you to stay with me after we leave this yacht. I want you to come live with me, not as my wife. As my woman.'

Her eyes searched his. 'For how long?'

'For as long as you like.'

She frowned. 'I can't promise to stay for ever, Mike.'

Mike knew exactly what she was saying. One day, she'd want more than he was willing to give her.

But that one day wasn't today, he thought with ruthless resolve as he pushed her back onto the bed.

'How long have we got before we have to get dressed for pre-dinner drinks?' he asked huskily as he wrapped her legs around him and thrust into her.

'About an hour,' she replied, moaning softly when he set up a powerful rhythm.

An hour. A day. A lifetime.

There would never be enough time, Mike realised on alternate waves of ecstasy and despair. Never!

# CHAPTER FIFTEEN

'WILL I do, darling?' Natalie asked as she paraded herself in front of Mike in her electric-blue party dress.

Mike's dark eyes blazed when they fastened on her cleavage.

'No,' he growled. 'You certainly won't do. You look much too sexy. Do you realise how many billionaires will be at this party tonight? Chuck told me he's flying in his super-rich friends from all over the world. There's sure to be some playboys amongst them who think nothing of seducing other men's wives.'

'Ah, but this wife is not in the market to be seduced,' Natalie purred as she sashayed up to Mike, who was looking pretty yummy himself in the same black dinner suit he'd worn at their wedding. 'She's way too satisfied with her husband.'

'Seduction is not always a matter of sex, Natalie,' he retorted. 'And what's with this *darling* business?'

She reached up on tiptoe to plant a soft kiss on his mouth. 'You don't like it?'

'I didn't say that. But it isn't quite you. It sounds…superficial.'

That was because he didn't realise she meant it, Natalie thought as she turned away and walked over to where she'd put her earrings. He *was* her darling. Her darling, and, with a bit of luck, the father of her baby.

And what will you do if you *have* fallen pregnant? Natalie wondered as she slipped her earrings into her lobes. Tell him, or just leave him without saying a word about it?

It would depend, she supposed, on how their relationship developed once they moved beyond the honeymoon phase.

But for now that honeymoon phase was exactly where they were at, and she was loving every delicious, decadent moment. Mike's need for sex with her still bordered on insatiable, his lovemaking ranging from slow and sensual to fast and furious. He couldn't seem to get enough, his desire often inflamed by what she was wearing. Or *not* wearing.

Her new wardrobe had been a fantastic success, especially the wicked black bikini Alanna had insisted she buy, and which she'd worn by the pool this morning. Mike hadn't been able to take his eyes off her. He'd been very impatient to get her back to the cabin, supposedly to change for lunch. The shower they'd had together had been rather long. He'd also loved the tight white Capri pants she'd worn for lunch, then lounging on deck afterwards, if the glitter in his eyes had been anything to go by. Though it was probably the skimpy red midriff top that had turned him on again, the one she'd worn with a bra.

Right at this moment, her only underwear was the tiniest G-string, bringing a sensual awareness of her body that was exquisitely exciting. The design of the dress heightened that awareness, the strapless bodice being ruthlessly boned, pulling her waist in and pushing her breasts up and together into a stunning cleavage. The bell-shaped skirt didn't touch her skin from her hips downwards, leaving room for air to swirl around her bare legs and mostly bare bottom.

'I hope you're at least wearing panties under that dress,' Mike muttered.

Natalie smiled a saucy smile at him in the wall mirror that hung over the dressing table. 'That's for me to know and you to find out.'

His groan was telling. So were his eyes.

Natalie liked nothing better than making Mike desperate with desire for her.

Maybe this was because she knew he didn't love her. His lust for her, however, was the next best thing. She could pretend that he loved her when he was inside her, when he cried out uncontrollably at the moment of his release, when his body trembled and shook with the force of his passion.

'What about these earrings?' she asked as she whirled back to face him, the rapid movement setting the long diamanté drops swinging back and forth across her bare shoulders. 'Too sexy as well?'

His smile was wry. 'You're trying to get a rise out of me.'

'Yes, indeed,' she said, her eyelashes fluttering before dropping down to his groin area.

He laughed. 'If only I'd known that first day how

naughty you were, I would have whisked you straight off to bed, like I wanted to.'

Natalie blinked her surprise. 'You wanted to take me to bed, even when I looked like a frump?'

'You'd better believe it.'

Nothing he'd ever said had pleased her so much.

'I wouldn't have said no,' she confessed as well.

'*Now* she tells me.'

'I didn't like you much, but I thought you were a sexy beast.'

'I do so love your backhanded compliments.'

She reached up to stroke his cheek. 'I like you much better now. In *every* way.'

He took a step back from her so that her hand dropped away.

'I think we should go up to the party, Natalie. Much as I don't like the idea of you being fancied by every man there, I don't want to risk ruining that very beautiful dress you're wearing. And I might, if we stay down here any longer.'

'I love it when you say things like that.'

'I know. Shall we go?'

'Goodness me,' Natalie murmured as they walked along the deck towards the main saloon. 'Sounds like there's a hundred people in there.'

Mike's hand tightened around hers. He hadn't been kidding when he'd said he was worried about some of the men at the party making a play for her. She looked extra desirable tonight in that glorious blue evening gown. Strapless dresses did become her, especially with her sexy new hairstyle. Mike loved the way it waved around her face and brushed sensually against her shoulders when she walked.

Other men would love it, too. Men far more handsome than he was. And far, far richer.

'Chuck said he'd invited a few extra guests at the last minute,' Natalie told him. 'Look, there's the launch coming in again now, bringing more people.'

They stopped at the railing, watching with interest as the launch angled itself against the *Rosalie* and a member of the crew set about helping the latest party-goers disembark.

'Hey, it's Rich and Reece!' Mike exclaimed, surprised and relieved when he recognised the two well-dressed and very handsome men as his friends.

'And Alanna and Holly,' Natalie added excitedly. 'Oh, don't they look lovely?'

Mike didn't think they held a candle to his Natalie, but they did look pretty good for very pregnant ladies. Alanna was wearing some long white floaty number and Holly was in black, with a silvery shawl around her shoulders.

They called out to each other and soon the six friends were gathered together on the deck, exchanging handshakes and hugs.

'This is a pleasant surprise,' Mike said. 'But a mystifying one. How come you're all here tonight?'

'Got an invite this afternoon,' Reece answered. 'Chuck decided after going past Palm Beach yesterday that he wanted to buy a house there. He rang one of his business contacts, asking him for the name of the best man in real estate in Sydney. Which was *moi*, of course.'

'Do try not to be so modest, darling,' Alanna said with a warm smile.

'Modesty never gets you anywhere,' Reece tossed off with his usual *savoir faire*. 'Anyway, Mike, I told Chuck we were great friends, whereupon he insisted I come to the party tonight, along with my better half. At that point I said if he really wanted to please you— and it seemed he did—then he'd invite Richard and Holly here as well.'

'After all,' Richard said. 'If Chuck buys a house here, he'll need a local banker, won't he?'

'What a pair of opportunists you are,' Mike said wryly. 'By the way, the partnership is in the bag, too.'

'That's great, Mike,' Richard congratulated. 'So it was worth getting married, was it?'

Worth it?

Mike thought of everything that had happened over the last few days. Then he thought of the future, and the day when Natalie would no longer be in his life.

'You don't honestly expect Mike to say that anything is worth getting married for,' Natalie broke in laughingly. 'But I don't think he's too miserable, are you, darling?' Her upward glance was downright wicked.

'*Darling*, no less,' Reece returned with a lift of his eyebrows. 'Sounds like you two have been enjoying a real honeymoon.'

'I think we'd better terminate this conversation,'

Richard said quietly. 'Chuck Helsinger is on the horizon, heading this way.'

Mike was grateful for Chuck's intervention. He wasn't in the mood to defend his relationship with Natalie. He also didn't want to keep examining his escalating feelings for her.

But that was exactly what he found himself doing over and over again during the next hour, especially when one of the billionaires at Chuck's lavish party did try to chat Natalie up. He was around fifty. Suave, handsome, and rich as Croesus. Married, of course. But that didn't stop him.

The moment Mike's back was turned to say something to Alanna, the lecherous devil invited Natalie for a dance out on the deck, where a band was playing and several couples were already locked in each other's arms.

A powerful jealousy claimed Mike as he watched Mr Moneybags wind his slimy arms around Natalie's bare back like some octopus. When he drew her much too close for Mike's liking, he knew he couldn't stand idly by.

'Hold this,' he said, shoving his glass of champagne into a startled Alanna's empty hand. 'My wife needs rescuing.'

Natalie was thinking how much she hated being out there, dancing with this oily creep, when Mike suddenly materialised, tapping her partner none too gently on his shoulder.

'My turn,' he announced, muscling in immediately

and whisking Natalie off into his arms, leaving Casanova in their wake with his mouth wide open.

As Mike twirled Natalie down the deck to a more private area she sighed her pleasure, and relief.

'What took you so long?' she said, her eyes sparkling up at him.

'I'm a bit slow sometimes.'

'Not that I've noticed,' she said cheekily. 'I see you're a good dancer, too.'

'You can thank Alanna for that. She taught me.'

This news startled her. And worried her, a bit. 'You like Alanna a lot, don't you?'

'She's a great girl.'

'You're not secretly in love with her, are you?'

'What? Don't be ridiculous!'

'She's very beautiful,' Natalie persisted, jealousy worming its unexpected way into her psyche.

'She's Reece's wife.'

'So?'

'Look, I'm not in love with Alanna, all right?' he said sharply. 'I told you. I don't fall in love.'

But even as he said the words Mike knew them to be a lie.

The realisation that he'd fallen in love with Natalie brought a maelstrom of emotions. First came a weird elation—he *could* love someone, after all—swiftly followed by something close to despair.

Because she didn't love him back. How could she? What was there to love about him?

She'd only agreed to stay in the marriage for a

while longer because of the sex. Once his partnership came through and she had her second million, she'd be off to make a life for herself with a nice, normal guy from a nice, normal background.

Mike didn't begrudge Natalie a happy life. Hell, he wanted her to be happy.

But Mike wasn't a masochist. He couldn't continue making love to her, knowing that he loved her. He was a man of extremes. It was all, or nothing.

So far in his life, there'd been nothing, emotionally.

Nothing, he could handle. Nothing, he could live with.

Love was too hard. Too gut-wrenching.

In the morning he would tell her it was over. Meanwhile, they had one more night together. Difficult to deny himself when they had to share a bed.

Difficult?

Near impossible!

That was why he had to get right away from her as soon as possible.

'What are you thinking about?'

Her quiet question startled him out of his thoughts.

'Do you really want to know?' he muttered against her hair, his arms tightening around her.

'Yes.'

He stopped dancing and stepped back to look down into her lovely blue eyes.

*I'm thinking that I would give anything to hear you say the three little words that I've always hated hearing on a woman's lips.*

'I was thinking about your underwear,' he lied. 'Or lack of it. *Do* you have panties on, my darling wife?'

When she flushed, his lie swiftly became the truth.

'I do, actually,' she returned breathily. 'But they're easily removed.'

Her continual eagerness to oblige him sexually both annoyed and aroused Mike. He could almost hate her when she was like this. It was so close to what he craved for. Yet so far away…

'Go and remove them,' he ordered her. 'Then come back to the main saloon. I'll be waiting for you there.'

'But…aren't you going to come to the cabin with me?'

'No.'

He was going to make her wait. And wait. And wait.

Tonight, he was going to be cruel. Tonight, he was going to punish her for making him love her.

He whirled her in his arms, pulling her back hard against him so that she could feel his erection, his mouth dipping to her right ear, his intention being to whisper the darkest of desires to her.

But when her head tipped softly to one side and a trembling sigh escaped her lips, his own lips did nothing but kiss her ear. Then her cheek. Her jawline. Her throat.

'Oh, Mike…'

His name on her lips was like a caress, making him melt.

How could he possibly hurt her? Or punish her?

He loved her.

He would show her how much tonight. With tenderness, not cruelty. If tonight was going to be his last night with her, he wanted to remember it with pride, not guilt, or shame.

Natalie was a wonderful woman. A special woman. She deserved the best he had to give.

'We really should get back to the party,' he said, his tone gentle. 'Don't worry about the panties for now. I'll take them off later tonight, when we're alone.'

# CHAPTER SIXTEEN

NATALIE woke to find Mike already up, fully dressed and packing.

'What…what are you doing?' she asked, pushing her hair out of her face as she sat up in the bed.

'Packing,' he replied. 'I thought that was obvious.'

His sharp tone shocked her. Where had the tender lover of last night gone to?

'But it's only eight-fifteen. We're not due to be dropped off at Darling Harbour till noon.'

His head lifted, his eyes hard and cold. 'I don't like to leave things to the last minute. Which brings me to something else.'

Natalie knew, before he said another word, that she wasn't going to like this something else.

'What?' she demanded to know, fear making her voice sharp as well.

'I've changed my mind, Natalie. Our living together isn't going to work for me. Sorry.'

Sorry.

Natalie's hands fell to the bed where she grasped at the sheet covering her lower half, holding onto it for dear life as she was holding onto her emotions for dear life.

Sorry.

One word, delivered without a care in the world.

Sorry.

One word, slashing into her heart and shattering all her hopes.

Of course, she'd been a fool to hope. But it was hard not to when the man you loved had made love to you half the night as if you were the most precious thing in the world to him and that he would never be able to live without you.

Sorry.

Her thoughts whirled as she tried to get her head around that one wretched word.

'For pity's sake, cover yourself up, would you?' Mike suddenly snapped.

Natalie blinked, then stared at him.

Cover herself up? This, from the man who had never been able to see enough of her. Who'd stripped her naked at every opportunity.

Suddenly, he was *offended* by the sight of her bared breasts? It didn't make sense.

Unless…

Dared she hope an even more outrageous hope?

Could it be possible?

'Why?' she asked him, leaving the sheet exactly where it was.

He scowled at her. 'What do you mean, why?'

'I mean why? Why do you want me to cover myself up all of a sudden? What are you afraid of?'

'I'm not afraid of anything,' he snarled.

'Then explain yourself. Last night was perfect between us. What's changed since then? You're a big one on telling the truth, Mike. But you're not telling me the truth now. I can feel it.'

'Can you just?'

'Yes,' she said, her eyes searching his.

He dragged his eyes away, slamming his case shut and zipping it up before glaring back at her.

'Don't be like all the others, Natalie. Don't make a bloody scene. Just accept what I say.'

'I'm not making a scene,' she countered. '*You're* the one making a scene. And I want to know why.'

'I'm going up on deck to have breakfast,' he told her harshly. 'You can please yourself what you do.'

Mike knew he had to get away.

Whirling, he strode swiftly towards the door, his hand lifting for the knob.

'You love me, don't you?'

Mike's hand froze in mid-air, his entire body stilling as well.

'That's what you're afraid of,' she threw at him. '*Loving* me.'

Mike closed his eyes for a moment. Then he turned, slowly, his insides churning, but his resolve strong. She wanted the truth. She would get the truth.

'No,' he denied. 'I'm not afraid of loving you. I'm afraid of hurting you. And of wasting your time. Yes, you're right. I do love you, Natalie. More than I ever thought possible. But you don't love me back. I know that. And I can understand why. I'm not a very lovable man. Far better you find someone you can love. Someone who'll give you everything you want, and deserve. A happy life. And children. You'd make a wonderful mother.'

'Oh, God,' she choked out, tears flooding her eyes.

'See what I mean? I've made you cry. And that's the last thing I wanted to do. I was trying to be cruel to be kind earlier. I was letting you go. But, like always, you couldn't let sleeping dogs lie, could you?'

'You don't understand,' she sobbed.

'What don't I understand? And, for pity's sake, *please* cover yourself up.'

Natalie scrambled to pull the sheet up, dabbing at her eyes whilst she struggled to find the right words to say to him. Her heart was so full. Of joy. And of fear.

How was he going to react when she told him she *did* love him? Would he believe her? And what about her possible pregnancy? He was sure to be angry with her, even if he did love her. Maybe he'd think she'd been trying to trap him all along. Oh God, she hoped not.

'But I *do* love you,' she blurted out.

His eyes widened, his face losing colour.

'Don't say that unless you mean it.'

'I do mean it. Oh, you've no idea how much I mean it.'

His face betrayed bewilderment. 'But you told Alanna over the phone it was just sex with you! I heard you.'

'I wanted to believe that was all I felt, because I thought you would never love me back. I was protecting myself.'

'You really love me?' he repeated, his expression still sceptical.

'Would I risk falling pregnant to you if I didn't?'

*'What?'*

'That day in the limousine. I lied to you. It wasn't a safe time for me. But it was a done deed, and once I realised I might have just conceived your baby I was so happy, Mike. I can't tell you how happy I was.'

'But you didn't know then that I loved you.'

'I was prepared to have your baby by myself, if I had to. Look, I haven't been trying to trap you, Mike. Honest. But I knew I wasn't going to fall in love again for a long, long time. And I wanted a child. Your child. Oh, please don't be angry with me. I know you always said you didn't want children, but I think you'd make a marvellous father. You have so much love to give, Mike. All you have to do is open your heart to the idea. And have faith in yourself. I have faith in you. You're a good man, Mike, even if you don't believe so yourself.'

She stopped talking at last, her heart pounding as she watched his face for his reaction.

Clearly, he was stunned. Then quietly thoughtful. When he started to walk back towards the bed, Natalie swallowed.

'You're not angry with me?' she choked out.

He sat down, his eyes no longer hard, or cold. He reached out to touch her face, wiping the tears from her cheeks with his fingertips.

'What are the chances of your being pregnant yet?' he asked softly.

'Um. Fair to middling.'

'But you might not be.'

'No,' she said, her heart squeezing tight. 'I…I might not be.' If he didn't want her to have his baby, she would just die!

'If you're not,' he said, a warm smile pulling at his mouth, 'we'll just have to keep trying, won't we?'

'Oh, Mike!' She dropped the sheet and threw her arms around him, kissing him. He kissed her back, for quite a long while.

'But we're going to have to make this marriage work,' he murmured as he pushed her back against the pillows. 'No child of mine is going to be raised by a single parent.'

'We'll make it work, Mike.'

'Yeah,' he said, his eyes shining as his head began to descend again. 'I reckon we will.'

## EPILOGUE

'YOU really don't mind that it's a girl?' Natalie asked Mike.

They hadn't wanted to know the sex of the baby beforehand. They'd liked the idea of it being a surprise.

Mike bent over the crib and smiled down into his sleeping daughter's lovely little face.

'Of course not,' he said. 'I'm just glad our baby's healthy and that you got through everything okay. You were so brave, opting for no epidural.'

'I wasn't that brave. I screamed my head off when she was coming out.'

'Yes, I can still hear you,' he said, patting his right ear. 'Do you think you could stand trying for a second after you've forgotten how awful it was?'

Natalie's heart turned over. And this was the man who'd never wanted children. Just seeing the look on his face the first time he'd held his newborn daughter had been worth all the pain in the world.

What a lovely man he was. A real softie underneath that tough, macho façade. Alanna had been right about that.

'It might cost you,' she said teasingly.

His head shot up. 'You mean I have to *pay* you to have another baby?'

'Not with cash.'

'What, then?'

'I want you to rent Chuck's boat for the week from Christmas till the New year. Tess will be three months old by then so I should be right and ready for a second honeymoon.'

'You do realise how much Chuck charges for that, don't you? Four hundred thousand a week! Next year we'd be able to afford it, but we've spent a small fortune this year buying that big house Reece found us. My program's only been on the market six months and it takes time for the money to come in.'

'Yes, I do know that. But there are six double cabins for guests on the *Rosalie*. We don't have to rent the boat alone. I've discussed it with Alanna and Holly. They said Reece and Richard will pay their fair share. Holly said Richard will want to bring his mother and stepfather, but they've got scads of money and would be only too happy to contribute. Alanna wants to invite her mother and her new husband as well. They don't have much money, but she's a fantastic cook. Reece's mother won't be coming. Apparently, she spends every Christmas with her youngest son and his family.'

'When on earth did you organise all this?' Mike asked.

'Oh…last week some time. So is it all right?'

'How can I refuse? That boat has a decidedly erotic effect on you. Must be all the rockin' and rollin'. But what about *your* parents? We can't leave them behind. Not at Christmas.'

'Heavens, no. Their coming with us is a foregone conclusion. And Dad can well afford to pay something, too. They're quite flush since you gave him the job of managing the Sydney office of Stoneware and Comproware Inc. That six-figure salary you and Chuck pay him is ridiculously generous, you know.'

'You have to be kidding. He's a bargain!'

'You mean he's really good at his job?'

'You'd better believe it. That man's a brilliant manager and he's darned clever with computers.'

'I didn't realise,' Natalie murmured.

'You've been too wrapped up in having the baby to notice anything else.'

'You're right,' she said, and cast an adoring glance over at her daughter. 'Could you pick her up for me, Mike? I want to hold her again.'

She watched as Mike carefully scooped his daughter up into his large arms, rocking her gently back and forth when she woke up and started crying.

'I think she's hungry,' he told Natalie as he handed her over.

Natalie rolled her eyes. 'Four hours old and you're already anticipating her needs. I suspect your daddy's going to spoil you rotten, Tess, my girl,' she murmured to her baby, who stopped crying when her mother put her little finger in her mouth to suck.

'That's why you need to have another baby quickly,' Mike said. 'So that I don't.'

'Children are a lot of work, you know. You should listen to Holly. Her Andrew's just started to walk and she says it's bedlam most of the time.'

'That's because he's a boy. Alanna's little girl is much quieter. And easier to handle.'

'*We* might have a boy next time.'

'I won't mind that. I'd call him Tony, after my little brother. The one who died of meningitis.'

Natalie could already feel herself melting. 'Tony's a nice name.'

'So's Tess,' Mike said, his voice sounding a bit choked up.

It suddenly came to Natalie why Mike wanted to call his daughter that particular name.

'Tess was your mother's name, wasn't it, Mike?' she said gently.

He looked away as he did sometimes, when his emotions threatened to embarrass him.

'Yeah. Yeah, it was.'

'You loved her a lot, didn't you?'

'Yeah. I did,' he admitted gruffly.

Natalie's stomach tightened when she glimpsed tears glistening in the corners of his eyes. 'She did love you, Mike. She loved you *and* Tony. She just couldn't cope.'

'You're probably right. She was very beautiful, you know.'

'I'm sure she was.'

'Little Tess looks a bit like her.'

'I'm glad.'

He turned his head back to face her and, yes, his eyes were definitely wet.

The noises of impending visitors coming down the hospital hallway stopped Natalie from crying herself.

It was her parents, their faces beaming, their arms full of flowers and gifts.

'Oh, isn't she just beautiful?' her mother gushed when Natalie handed her daughter over to her grandmother. 'Look, John.'

'A real beauty,' her grandfather agreed. 'What are you going to call her?'

'Tess,' Mike answered, then added quite loudly and proudly, 'She's named after my mother.'

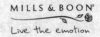

MILLS & BOON®  1105/01b

*Live the emotion*

# Modern
## romance™

### THE ITALIAN'S CONVENIENT WIFE
*by Catherine Spencer*

When Paolo Rainero's niece and nephew are orphaned
he must protect them.  A marriage of convenience to
Caroline Leighton, their aunt, is his solution.  But he must
show Callie that he's changed since their fling nine years
ago.  Their mutual desire is rekindled – but Paolo feels
that Caroline has a secret…

### THE ANTONAKOS MARRIAGE *by Kate Walker*

An ageing tycoon is blackmailing Skye Marston into
marriage – but she'll have one night of passion first…
Theo Antonakos is furious when she slips away from him
– and still furious when he goes to meet his stepmother-
to-be.  Only to find that they already know each other
– in the most intimate way…

### MISTRESS TO A RICH MAN *by Kathryn Ross*

Celebrity agent Marc Clayton knows a gold-digger when
he sees one.  And when gorgeous Libby Sheridan shows
up, to cause a scandal for his top client, he knows he
needs to keep her close – *very* close…  Libby won't be
bought off – but as their power struggle turns to passion
Marc takes her out of the limelight…and into his bed!

### TAMED BY HER HUSBAND *by Elizabeth Power*

Everyone thinks they know Shannon Bouvier – heiress,
wild child, scandalous man-eater.  And she's happy to let
the world believe the lies.  Kane Falconer thinks he knows
her too. It's his job to tame Shannon – and this ruthless
millionaire knows just how…

## On sale 2nd December 2005

*Available at most branches of WHSmith, Tesco, ASDA,*
*Borders, Eason, Sainsbury's and most bookshops*

Visit www.millsandboon.co.uk

# *Experience the magic of Christmas, past and present...*

# *Christmas Brides*

### *Don't miss this special holiday volume – two captivating love stories set in very different times.*

## THE GREEK'S CHRISTMAS BRIDE
### by Lucy Monroe
### Modern Romance

Aristide Kouros has no memory of life with his beautiful wife Eden. Though she's heartbroken he does not remember their passion for each other, Eden still loves her husband. But what secret is she hiding that might bind Aristide to her forever – whether he remembers her or not?

## MOONLIGHT AND MISTLETOE
### by Louise Allen
### Historical Romance – Regency

From her first night in her new home in a charming English village, Hester is plagued by intrusive "hauntings." With the help of her handsome neighbour, the Earl of Buckland, she sets out to discover the mystery behind the frightful encounters – while fighting her own fear of falling in love with the earl.

## On sale 4th November 2005

# FREE

## 4 BOOKS AND A SURPRISE GIFT!

We would like to take this opportunity to thank you for reading this Mills & Boon® book by offering you the chance to take FOUR more specially selected titles from the Modern Romance™ series absolutely FREE! We're also making this offer to introduce you to the benefits of the Reader Service™—

★ **FREE home delivery**
★ **FREE gifts and competitions**
★ **FREE monthly Newsletter**
★ **Books available before they're in the shops**
★ **Exclusive Reader Service offers**

Accepting these FREE books and gift places you under no obligation to buy; you may cancel at any time, even after receiving your free shipment. Simply complete your details below and return the entire page to the address below. You don't even need a stamp!

**YES!** Please send me 4 free Modern Romance books and a surprise gift. I understand that unless you hear from me, I will receive 6 superb new titles every month for just £2.75 each, postage and packing free. I am under no obligation to purchase any books and may cancel my subscription at any time. The free books and gift will be mine to keep in any case.

P5ZEE

Ms/Mrs/Miss/Mr..........................................Initials ...............................
**BLOCK CAPITALS PLEASE**

Surname ..............................................................................................

Address ...............................................................................................

.............................................................................................................

.............................................................Postcode ...............................

Send this whole page to:
The Reader Service, FREEPOST CN81, Croydon, CR9 3WZ